FOREVER SUNRISE
A RIVER TO IMMORTALITY

A Science Fiction Adventure Novel
by
Stephen Chase

Contents

1. Gwen   1

2. The Infirmary   4

3. Three Peaks   7

4. Akio   18

5. The Naiporos   22

6. Nine Years Later   26

7. The Expo   33

8. CBT Session Two   50

9. Itsy   54

10. CBT Ten   57

11. Grad School   60

12. Dissertation   71

13. The River of No Return   75

14. Gwen's Laboratory   84

15. The Peacock   91

16. Up the River, One   96

17. Up the River, Two   99

18. Up the River, Three   103

19. Hatchery 1>4666   110

20. GenLife   121

21. The Throne   129

22. Canada   135

23. The Party of Amaterasu   138

24. Surprise at the Peacock   142

25. The Vote   145

26. Matsutake   146

27. The Reception   151

28. In Vitro   155

29. Prince Hitomu   157

30. The Hunt   160

31. Wire Tokyo   167

32. Discovery   171

33. Why   176

34. Ethics   180

35. Three Years Later   184

Many thanks to the Vero Beach, Florida Tuesday Writers, author and editor Jeanne Selander Miller and Kathryn C. Chase, Patricia Schiller, and Caitlin Regan for all their encouragement and help.

Cover art by Jamie Sale.

Author's Note

AS AN EMERGENCY MEDICINE PHYSICIAN FOR FORTY-FIVE YEARS, I've often encountered death and maladies related to aging. I've met very few people who looked forward to experiencing either of those certainties. What if science surprises us again? What if aging and death could be prevented? How many would line up for the shot? Would you be one? My first novel, **FOREVER SUNRISE**, might help you make that decision.

IN THE 1800s, Jules Verne wrote fictional stories about men going to the moon. *Forever Sunrise* is a fictional story about a young scientist's quest for immortality. Pundits will criticize the science in this novel as flawed, as pure fiction. They're right. Forever Sunrise is fiction . . . or maybe not.

1. Gwen

AS A CROCUS PEEKS ITS HEAD OUT OF THE SNOW TO ANNOUNCE the spring, music class was the harbinger of the weekend. Every Friday of the school year, Mrs. Helminiak changed from teacher to maestro. She sat behind her enormous oak desk which dominated the front of the class-room. It was her command post, the symbol of her superiority. She was the teacher; they were the children. From her swivel chair behind the desk, she could read from her notes, spin around to write on the chalkboard or stare down any child who considered misbehaving. The twenty-four children sat in little desks lined up in four rows facing their teacher. Seats closest to her were earned by misbehaving students.

Gwen's behavior had always been exemplary. She had earned a seat farther back in the classroom. The fond memories Gwen retained from her childhood on the reserve came from September days like this: bright sunshine, the aroma of autumn air, her friends, music class, and the weekend ahead. In 1991, Gwendolyn Sunrise was a fourth-grader at the Three Peaks First Nations Elementary School in British Columbia.

On cue from the intercom buzzer announcing last period, Mrs. Helminiak arose from her chair. Her enlarged, middle-aged figure waddled six steps around her fortress to stand in front of the class. She stood motionless as a mime imitating a statue. She held a black baton high in front of her right shoulder. Every child knew this posture signaled absolute quiet. They awaited her signal to start singing. An almost imperceptible upward nod of her head preceded a downward thrust of the baton. It now pointed to the middle of the first row. Her silent lips mimicked

1

the word "Row." On cue, the children in that row began singing, "Row, row, row your boat gently down the stream." When they sang the word "stream," the baton moved to Gwen's row. They started harmonizing, "Row, row, row your boat," as the first row sang, "Merrily, merrily, merrily, merrily, life is but a dream." The remaining children followed in sequence until all four rows and all four stanzas melded together.

The class was excellent, on key, harmonizing the repetitive stanzas. As if looking at a hypnotist's swinging watch, Gwen drifted from the present into a world of her own. She became focused on the words, "Life is but a dream." Gwen was about to experience her first confrontation with the reality of her own mortality.

The words grew louder and louder in her head until they began to shout at her. "Life is but a dream. Life is but a dream." Life, a dream? She knew what dreams were. They vanish when she awakened. She remembered some of her dreams; floating away from her mother and father, reaching out for their hands and missing as they disappeared into the darkness. They were horrible, frightening nightmares, ending when she awakened crying. Now, she thought, *When I die will my life just disappear, like a dream? Merrily row your boat through life until your dream ends, until everything is nothing; no more playing, no more friends, no more mother, no more father, no more eyes, no more feet. Her heart raced and pounded. No, no, no, I don't want to die. I don't want nothingness forever. I love my life. I love my friends. I love my mother and father.* She screamed, "I don't want to die. I don't want to die!" until Mrs. Helminiak's voice pulled her back into reality. The terrifying vision ended. Her lifelong fear of death began.

"Gwen, it's all right," Mrs. Helminiak said, wiping Gwen's drenched brow with a hand-kerchief. "You're alive. You're in school. All your friends are here. You're okay." She took Gwen by the hand, turned to the frightened class, and announced, "Class,

Gwen is fine. She had a bad dream. You may be dismissed now. Enjoy your weekend. We'll talk about this on Monday."

"Gwen, let's walk over to the clinic and see if Nurse Dawn has something to help you feel better."

2. The Infirmary

As they walked across the village towards the Three Peaks Medical Clinic, Mrs. Helminiak held Gwen's hand and told her stories of her own childhood fears. No different from most children who experience a meltdown, Gwen was feeling much better by the time they arrived. As embarrassing as the episode could have been, it caused this nine-year-old little concern. It was the weekend and she had more important things to do. Her friends would be waiting at home to play. Death could wait. She had an entire life ahead to solve the problem.

After a brief conversation with Nurse Dawn, she asked Gwen to sit in the waiting room. Dawn held two positions: school nurse and clinic nurse. Gwen and her friends didn't know if Dawn was her first name, nickname, last name, or both. It didn't matter; the children liked her. She grew up in their village along the Skeena River as it coursed through the midwestern part of British Columbia. When she returned from the University of Northern British Columbia with a nursing degree, she wanted to serve and give back to her own people whose ancestors had thrived as well as struggled on this land for ten thousand years.

Gwen looked around the dreary waiting room. Two adult patients sat on scratched, folding chairs, ignoring the white noise of an afternoon game show coming from a wall-mounted TV. A cracked pine table holding several ripped, outdated magazines stood alone against one wall. Gwen noticed a rack on the wall holding pamphlets. She saw pictures of people smoking and sticking needles into their arms. She didn't understand others. One read, HIV in big letters. Alone on a small table sat a box labeled "Free Condoms." She assumed condoms were a type of candy. To her disappointment, the box was empty.

It wasn't long before Nurse Dawn beckoned, "This way to the examining room, Wendy." Wendy was a nickname some people called her. Her family preferred Gwen or Gwendolyn. Her little brother, Peter, called her "Wen-Wen." She responded to them all. "Sit here, please," Nurse Dawn said, pointing to a chair next to a stainless steel cabinet containing tongue depressors and other medical paraphernalia.

"Are you feeling better?"

Gwen nodded yes. She was glad Nurse Chalmers wasn't there. One of the children in her class said she overheard her parents saying Chalmers was a "monster nurse." Gwen had never met her, but her friends said she was worse than any disease she treated.

"Death can be a scary thought," said Nurse Dawn.

Gwen looked at the floor while Dawn took her pulse and temperature. "Stick out your tongue and say, ahh." After excusing herself for a few minutes, Dawn returned with a small glass of milk and a cookie. "Your father will be here soon."

Gwen heard a conversation outside the door using the words "stream, dream, die, okay, and thank you for coming, Frank." She assumed Dawn was talking to her father. As he walked through the doorway into the examining room, he gave Gwen an approving nod which expressed more than words. She could read the happiness on her father's face. Nurse Dawn had reassured him his daughter wasn't ill. Having come from work, he still wore his steel-toed boots and greasy, blue uniform from his job as a large truck mechanic. His chiseled facial features and long, straight black hair typified many pure-blooded First Nations men. Some of Gwen's friends would have been more fearful of facing their fathers than facing their first confrontation with death. Not Gwen, he caressed her hair and put a gentle hand on her shoulder before leading her to his pickup truck for the short drive home.

"Are you feeling better now?" was all he asked.

"Yes, Father. I was very scared."

"Tomorrow morning, we can talk more about it. We'll saddle up Gypsy and ride to Sparkle."

3. Three Peaks

GWEN JUMPED OUT OF HER FATHER'S TRUCK AND RACED UP THE three steps of the porch into her mother's arms. Being a teacher at Regional High School, Mary was also happy to be out of school for the weekend. Gwen thought her mother was pretty. She didn't notice any differences between her mother and most of the other mothers living at Three Peaks. The adults noticed. If the maiden name Mary Connolly didn't give away her ethnicity, her auburn hair, fair skin, and blue eyes did. After teaching several years in the Boston suburbs, Mary decided to add a bit of adventure to her life. A job-posting from a First Nations grammar school in Prince Rupert, British Columbia, caught her eye. They accepted her application after considerable red tape due to her U.S. citizenship.

During one school vacation week while teaching in Canada, she took a rafting trip down the Babine River in north central British Columbia. Mary fell in love with her Indigenous guide, Frank Sunrise; one thing led to another and they married four years later.

Frank and Mary knew everyone wouldn't accept their marriage. Marriages between Natives and non-Natives used to be taboo. Now they were becoming more frequent. Some First Nations prohibited mixed couples from living on the res. Although Three Peaks encouraged their members to marry Native, most were accepting of all people. As newlyweds, they chose to live on the land of Frank's ancestry, enjoying its spiritual and financial advantages.

"Mother, may I run over to Skyla's house to play?"

"Yes, and come back for dinner in one hour. Do you have your watch?"

"Yes, Mother, I'll be back on time."

When Gwen stepped out of her front door, she looked over a short flood plain separating her house from a broad section of the Skeena River. The sounds of water tumbling over rocks greeted her. The river flowed downstream from its origin 250 kilometers northwest in the Spatsizi Plateau. After passing Three Peaks, it continued the same distance southeast to empty into the Pacific Ocean. The river was in Gwen's blood. It was part of her people's lifeline, providing food, transportation, and commerce throughout their history. Looking ten kilometers beyond the opposite river bank, she could see three majestic, glacier-capped mountains. Those peaks spiritually bound her Three Peaks Nation to the area for over ten thousand years, and Gwen, for the rest of her life.

Skipping down a zigzag dirt road, she passed many homes on her way to Skyla's house. Too young to see the poverty suffered by many of her people, Gwen saw small, one or two-story wood dwellings topped with tin or asphalt roofs. When she grew older, she learned the differences between each house reflected more the owner's personality than their income. A low, white picket fence surrounded the Sunrise's small property. They maintained a vegetable garden, a flower garden, a horse, and had two older-model pick-up trucks. The floors in their house were clean, the kitchen spotless, the beds made, the furniture, and appliances maintained. Their one-level house announced they weren't rich, but they took pride in what they had.

When Gwen reached Skyla's house, she saw dirt-coated windows, wrecked cars, and odd bits of construction material littering the yard.

"Hickety Pickety Pop,
Hickety Pickety Pop,
How many times before I stop?
1, 2, 3."

Two other fourth grade girls were jumping rope with Skyla on the sand road in front of her yard. Skyla knew better than to invite her friends any closer to her property. Only their friend, Karen, had ever been invited into the house. Both of Karen's parents were Indigenous. As soon as Gwen arrived, Skyla's father, Joe Blackstone, kicked open the ripped screen door with his boot, emerged, and stood along the front deck rail. With arms folded and a frown on his face, he glared at the children, particularly at Gwen. She dropped her gaze and looked away. Somehow Gwen knew it was her blue eyes and lighter complexion that offended him. None of the children ever talked with him. None of them had seen Skyla's mother. No one dared ask.

The children rotated their positions between taking turns between being one of the rope twirlers and one of the jumpers. None of the little girls mentioned Gwen's episode in school. Gwen, too, had pushed the incident from her mind.

"Teacher, teacher,
What did I get?
What did I get on my spelling test?
A, B, C."

The girls twirling the jump rope sang along as the other girls took turns jumping in.

"Doctor, doctor,
Shall I die?

9

Yes, my darling,
Bye and bye."

That verse caught Gwen's attention for a fleeting moment before she dismissed it without further thought. The girls continued skipping rope for about thirty minutes.

"Fudge, fudge,
Call the judge,
Skyla's goin' to have a baby.
Her boyfriend's going crazy.
How many babies
1, 2, 3."

Although the children had little understanding of the words' significance, the last rhyme pushed Big Joe over the top. The children could see the anger on his face as he yelled, "Skyla, get in here right in, now." She obeyed without hesitation.

Later in life, Gwen learned that Big Joe resented anybody of mixed blood. Despite having grown up with Gwen's father, when Frank Sunrise married outside the Nation, Big Joe disassociated himself from him. Gwen's blue eyes fanned the embers of his smoldering hatred. Gwen heard her parents talking one night about Joe. He had been the class bully, dropping out of school as early as the law permitted. His marriage ended in scandal. His verbal and physical abuse towards his wife forced her to leave the reserve. In those days, before the criteria for defining Indian status had been modernized, she lost her status and government benefits. Joe, being the male, retained his. Skyla was their only child.

Skyla's father scared Gwen. She looked at her watch and was happy to walk home. Dinner was on the table. She could smell the freshly grilled steelhead their neighbor had caught in the morning. Gwen was hungry.

"Where's Father?" Gwen asked.

"He's working late this evening."

Gwen joined Mother and Peter at the table. Mother started by chanting a brief blessing usually given by Frank. During their courtship, Mary became enthralled with First Nations culture and knew more about it than many of the locals.

Although Gwen had forgotten about her episode in school, her mother already knew. Word traveled fast in a small community.

"I understand you had a bad dream in school today."

Gwen didn't know what to say. She remained quiet.

"What was your dream about?"

Gwen's shoulder shrug denoting ignorance didn't set her free, nor did Peter's behavior. At four-years-old, he enjoyed instigating his Mother's disapproval by playing with his toy racing car on the dinner table. Distraction over, Gwen again found herself on the spot. In a calm voice, Mary persisted, "What part scared you?"

"Dying," Gwen whispered.

"Who dying?" Mary asked as she reached across the table for her daughter's hand.

"Me, you, Father, Peter."

Mary paused before continuing. "What made you think of that?"

"We were singing, 'Row, row, row your boat.' It said life is just a dream."

"It's only a nursery rhyme, just little song. Why did it bother you?"

"What happens to us when we die, Mother?"

While passing Peter his plate of food, she said, "God will

take care of us. He made the earth, the trees, the mountains, the oceans, and all the creatures. Because many people became evil, God sent His son, Jesus, to earth to save us all. If you are good, when you die, you will go to heaven and be happy forever living with God and Jesus."

"Will you, Father, Peter, Grandmother, and all my friends be in heaven with me?"

"We'll all be there."

With a gesture of relief, Gwen exhaled. Death didn't sound bad to her after all.

As promised, Frank woke Gwen the next morning for a ride on Gypsy to Sparkle Lake. Their horse, Gypsy, measured fourteen hands high. A distinguishing white stripe extended from the top of her forehead to her nose. Her gentleness made her more a family pet than a horse.

Frank helped Gwen up and onto Gypsy's back before mounting the saddle to sit behind his daughter. Allowing Gwen to hold the reins made her feel she had control. In reality, Gypsy needed no control. She knew the three-kilometer route passing in front of the police and fire departments, the Salvation Army, utility buildings, and the gas station. Gypsy knew to stop at the entry sign which read *Three Peaks First Nations Reserve*. Frank's light tap of his heels signaled a safe time to cross the undivided, two-lane highway. A short distance beyond, they continued down a dirt path, through a pasture, along a pine and spruce-lined forest, and up a hill to the trailhead leading to Sparkle Lake. They rode without talking. Listening to the hypnotic, clip-clop sounds of hooves and smelling the aroma of pine needles, needed no human elaboration.

From the trailhead parking lot, they looked down at a

beautiful vista leading through Sparkle Valley. The hard-packed lot sometimes served as a hangout for local teenagers seeking refuge from authority. Frank felt the strewn cigarette butts, beer cans, empty nips, and candy wrappers reflected some youths' disregard for the earth. He looked up and apologized to Mother Earth for their behavior.

As usual, he had brought a plastic garbage bag. After dismounting and tying Gypsy's reins to a split-rail fence, he and Gwen picked up trash before riding on.

At the entrance to the trailhead from the parking lot a staked sign read:

Three Peaks Nation
No Trespassing Without A Permit

Three Peaks Nation was one of about two hundred different Indigenous Nations in British Columbia. Being the oldest of Three Peaks Nation's six villages, Gwen's village shared its Nation's name. Each of the other five villages in the Nation had their own name.

They rode Gypsy out of the parking lot and switched-back down a steep hillside trail into Sparkle Valley. After about a kilometer, they passed the band's cemetery. A weather-beaten, wooden sign read:

Three Peaks Burial Grounds
Sacred Land
No Trespassing

After riding another kilometer, they arrived at Sparkle Lake. One of the hundreds of pristine lakes scattered throughout British Columbia, Sparkle formed an irregular ellipse spanning about five kilometers in length by two kilometers wide. Frank never tired of looking at its dark blue, crystal-clear water splashing against the rock, gravel, and sand shoreline. As he gazed around the lake, he saw tall spruce abutting the shore. In the distance, the valley rose into hills before climbing to subalpine fir and pine-covered mountains.

As a member of the band council governing Three Peaks, Frank had spent countless hours fending off development schemes by oil diggers and tree cutters. Sparkle Lake belonged to his Nation.

He dragged an aluminum canoe from a hiding place in the brush to the water's edge. One at a time, Gwen carried the paddles. After digging for worms and letting Gypsy drink, they loaded the canoe. Frank's strong strokes from the stern fooled Gwen into thinking her paddling motions helped propel the canoe. When they reached a favorite spot, her father rigged their two collapsable fishing poles. Gwen was proud she knew how to bait her hook.

"Let's see how many different living things we can see today," said Frank, suggesting a game they had often played.

He pointed at Gwen and himself. "Two people, now it's your turn, Gwendolyn."

"Worms, here in the old tin can," she said, with a proud smile.

They alternated, calling out the names of wildlife. A hawk descended to about thirty meters above the water and hovered before diving down to plunge its talons deep into the water.

"Hawk," said Frank, pointing.

It emerged with a bass and flew high into the firs.

"Fish," Gwen shouted.

After a while, Frank changed the rules, "Let's see if we can name things the hawk needs to live. I'll start with the air it needs

14

to breathe and fly."

Gwen loved the games her father played with her. She didn't realize they were teaching exercises. They named air, earth, sun, trees, and water before Gwen ran out of answers.

Frank's tone became more serious. "An insect eating a leaf falls to the ground. It's eaten by a frog. The frog jumps into the water. It's eaten by a little fish which is eaten by a bigger fish. Mother hawk dives down and catches the big fish in its talons. She flies to her nest on top of a tall tree, feeds her babies, and eats the rest herself. After the babies grow and can fly away from their nest, mother hawk becomes old and sick. One day, she stands on the ground and dies."

"What happens to mother hawk when she dies?" asked Gwen after a brief silence.

"Her body goes into the ground. Over many years it becomes part of the soil, which feeds the tree, so it can grow tall. When one of her baby hawks grows up, it flies to the top of the tree and builds a nest."

"Where does mother hawk go when she dies?"

"Her spirit leaves her and lives forever as part of the Circle of Life."

Gwen didn't grasp the whole meaning of what her father said. As life went on, she understood a little more each time he spoke about the Circle of Life, the Creator, and Mother Earth. She learned from her culture to honor all forms of life as her sisters and brothers. Her parents taught her to respect the earth, the sun, the air, the water, the plants, and the animals. "People are only one part," Frank would say before quoting Chief Seattle: "The earth does not belong to man; man belongs to the earth."

They fished a few more spots without bites. After paddling back to shore, hiding the canoe, and packing up Gypsy's saddlebag, they started the ride back home. As Gwen's long black braids bounced to Gypsy's cadence, they rode over only one small footprint of the 30,000 square miles of land stolen from their ancestors by gold seekers, oil drillers, and loggers.

Before climbing the hill to the parking lot, they dismounted at the tribal cemetery. A waist-high wooden picket fence surrounded its one acre periphery. Plastered against it were old ribbon fragments blown there by the wind. If the grave markers could have talked, they would have told how the white man's epidemics killed the people buried below. Family totems would have wept as they remembered when their children were forced to leave for an education designed to convert them from being savages. Modern headstones would have cried out to apologize to those buried beneath them for allowing them to have been proselytized away from their traditional ways and spiritual beliefs.

Frank and Gwen walked in silence to the Sunrise family plot, a square area he had demarcated with stones. "These are the graves of my father, grandmother, grandfather, and baby sister," said Father while standing with his eyes closed. He lifted his arms towards the sky, as if to invite the sky to join him, and chanted a prayer to the dead in the ancient language of his People. Gwen had seen her father perform this ritual before. She knew she needed to stand still and be quiet.

"What happens to me when I die?" Gwen asked after her father had finished.

"You never will die. Like Mother Hawk, your spirit will leave your body and travel to the world of all our people. We are now walking among the spirits. They're always looking after us. Someday, we will join them. I called upon the spirits and asked them to save your mother, me, Peter, and you a place with them when the time comes."

Gwen felt relieved to know she still would be together with her family when she died. The only problem facing her now was, no matter how hard she tried, she couldn't see the spirits.

Before continuing home, they stopped at the trailhead to pick up their trash bag. Gwen felt reassured now having heard two explanations of death as a continuation of her happy life. She could put her fears to rest, for now.

She thought little about death until her second year of college when she started questioning her childhood beliefs.

4. Akio

DURING THE SAME YEAR OF 1991, WHEN DEATH BECAME PERSONAL to Gwen Sunrise, an eleven-year-old sixth-grader named Akio Naiporo walked from his family's apartment to South Elementary School in Shisaman City. Located on the southeast Pacific coast of Hokkaido, Japan, this austere, working-class city had a population of 20,000.

Carrying a book bag on his back, he stepped through the school's main entrance. After exchanging street shoes for comfortable white cloth sneakers, he placed his shoes and red hat neatly into a cubby. Akio wore blue jeans and his favorite Selbu Lions baseball team shirt. His school didn't require uniforms.

Sixty percent of the students in Akio's school descended from indigenous Ainu ancestry. The remaining forty percent were ethnic-majority Japanese. Akio was one-quarter Ainu.

Today, the children ate a hot lunch of rice, fish, and soup inside their classroom. After lunch, all thirty-five moved into small groups for cleanup. Each child knew his or her specific job. This week, Akio's group carried the dirty plates to the kitchen. A spotless classroom greeted their teacher when she returned from her lunch break.

History class followed lunch. The young teacher, Miss Sato, played a black and white tape on the VCR. It began with a picture of a Japanese family huddled beside their radio. Through considerable static, they listened to the Emperor's August 15, 1945, surrender speech.

The tape's narrator announced, "This is the first time in Japan's history His subjects had heard the Divine voice of an

Emperor."

His Imperial Majesty spoke:

"To Our good and loyal subjects: After pondering
deeply the general trends of the world and the
actual conditions obtaining to Our Empire today,
We have decided to effect a settlement of the
present situation by resorting to an extraordinary
measure. We have ordered Our government to
communicate to the governments of the United
States, Great Britain, China, and the Soviet Union
that Our Empire accepts the provisions of their
Joint Declaration."

The tape skipped to another part of the Emperor's
statement,

"My ties with the people do not depend upon
mere legends and myths. They are not predicated
on the false conception that the Emperor is Divine
and that the Japanese people are superior to other
races."

Miss Sato turned off the VCR and announced, "Class,
we'll now split up into our seven groups."

The children moved their chairs into small circles. Every
Monday, a new group list appeared on the bulletin board. Giggles
heard from certain girls meant their names appeared in a group
with a boy they liked. Akio sat in a circle with one boy and three
girls. Being the tallest boy in his class and thought to be handsome
by many girls, all three girls in his group giggled. Miss Sato wrote
questions on the chalkboard:

19

1. Why did the Emperor give the speech?
2. What does "the Emperor is divine" mean?
3. Do you think the Emperor is divine?

She instructed, "Discuss these questions among your groups. Choose a spokesperson. In twenty minutes, you'll stop and voice your opinions. Remember, there are no right or wrong answers, just opinions."

The groups went to work. A low-pitched din of conversation permeated the classroom. They had previously studied the history of World War II. It ended thirty-five years before these children were born. They learned the Emperor at the time was Emperor Hirohito. As Japanese tradition demands, posthumously, he is referred to by a different name he'd chosen during his reign, Emperor Shöwa. When the allotted time had elapsed, each group delivered an opinion. The confused look on some of the students' faces reflected the difficulty of this exercise for sixth graders. Miss Sato helped guide them.

Akio was the spokesperson for the last group's presentation. After bowing to Miss Sato, he started, "Sensei, four of us thought the Emperor surrendered because he loved Japan and wanted to save more people from being killed by atomic bombs. We all agreed 'divine' means all the emperors of Japan are gods. The sun-goddess, Amaterasu, sent them to us."

Akio didn't feel nervous talking in front of the class. Miss Sato once wrote on his quarterly evaluation report for parents, *He is popular and confident without a hint of arrogance.*

"And did your group think the Emperor was a god?"

"We had different opinions. Three were sure the Emperor was a god. That's what their parents had told them. They thought the Americans forced the Emperor to say he wasn't. One said he wasn't, and one didn't know."

"What was your opinion, Akio?"

"My mother thinks he was a god, like all the emperors before him. My father believes no man is a god. I was the one who didn't know."

"Thank you, class. You did excellent work today."

After carrying their chairs back to their desks, the students changed into street shoes or sneakers before lining up at the door. Their smiles left no doubt—sports was next.

5. The Naiporos

AKIO SPENT THE NEXT DAY WITH HIS FATHER. SCHOOL HAD offered parents the opportunity to take their children to work with them. Little did this eleven-year-old realize his visit to the Shisaman South Salmon Hatchery would lay the foundation for one of the most challenging experiences he would encounter in life.

That evening, the Naiporos sat down for dinner. At age eleven, Akio would have preferred to play baseball, but he knew joining his mother's Shinto ceremonies gave her pleasure. Mrs. Naiporo stood up from her chair at the dining table to walk towards the southeast corner of their living room. The 38 year-old, petite woman looked up at her kamidana sitting on the top shelf of a bookcase. This personal shrine, about the size of a dollhouse, contained a wooden centerpiece resembling a clothes closet with two vertical doors. Hidden inside was an ofuda, a white card that had been empowered by her local shrine to connect worshippers with gods and spirits. Shinto taught her everything in life contains a kami or a spiritual essence. At death, one's kami is released to another world, able to return to connect with the living. In front of the kamidana stood white saucers, bowls, and jars holding sake, salt, rice, and water for the spirits.

Akio's older sister, Yuri, stood next to him in front of the kamidana. They bowed twice and clapped their hands twice. Mother prayed out loud, "Thank you, immortal spirits of our ancestors and the great sun goddess, Amaterasu, for visiting us from the land of the gods. May you protect our family, our house, and the food on our table." Mother's clap signaled the ritual's end.

22

The family ate in silence until Grandfather started the conversation.

"What did you learn today at the hatchery, Akio?"

Akio's mind flashed back to sitting beside three other students on the hatchery's observation platform. He looked down onto the Shisaman River tumbling over a low dam into a pond. As the rising sun's beams illuminated the pond, men dressed in chest-high waders worn over layers of clothing entered the cold water. Over the sound of the river, Akio could hear his father's voice instructing each man where to drag his section of an expansive fishnet.

"Father works hard. Watching him net salmon in cold water made me appreciate him even more."

Father acknowledged the compliment with a shallow, expressionless nod.

"Anything else?" asked Grandfather.

After pausing to think, Akio said, "Well, Grandfather, I never knew salmon die right after they spawn."

The Naiporo dinners differed from many families. Yuri and Akio were encouraged and felt comfortable joining the adults in respectful conversation.

Yuri commented, "I just learned, in Professor Tonegawa's biology class, salmon grow tired after swimming all the way from the ocean to where they spawn. Right after they spawn, they run out of gas and die." Being the first child in the Naiporo family to continue beyond high school, Yuri's rapid speech reflected her excitement at showing her parents what she had learned during her first year at Hokkaido University. She wanted her family to see all that she was learning. It was her way of thanking them for their sacrifices.

Mrs. Naiporo glanced at her husband, waiting to see if he wanted to speak. When he remained quiet, she said, "There's no mystery. Salmon follow the way of all life. The young replace the old. Their spirits join the immortal spirits of all things."

When Grandfather heard the word "salmon," his mind's tape recorder started to play one of his often-told stories. They usually concerned his personal experiences rather than answers to any specific question. He reminisced, "Salmon gave us Ainu people food for thousands of years. When I was a boy growing up in North Hokkaido, my father used to take me out on the rivers to spear salmon. After I married and moved here, I worked in the Hokkaido Mushroom Factory and..."

Grandfather would have rambled on and on had he not paused to take a sip of miso soup. Hoping not to insult his father, Mr. Naiporo took advantage of the interruption to speak. "Akio-san, what else interested you today?"

Akio saw something which he felt uneasy discussing. His father's question gave him an opening. "Otosan, I liked seeing the men milk eggs from the salmon and the little fish in tanks jumping. I didn't understand was why people who looked like they were Ainu, did all the dirty work. The others, including Doctor Kubo, wore nice clothes and worked in offices."

Father didn't answer right away. He had to think. The Naiporos hadn't discussed prejudice with Akio and Yuri. They felt having them experience it would be a better teacher.

"We need to have a talk about prejudice. Let's discuss it later," said Mr. Naiporo.

Sitting in the living room area after dinner, Grandfather fell asleep in his comfortable chair. If awake, when he heard the word "prejudice," he would have lectured on how the Ainu were the original people of Hokkaido, living on its rich, unspoiled land for thousands of years before others arrived from the South. He would have told stories how the Ainu culture became plagued by non-acceptance and conflict. Negative stereotypes abounded, such as poor, dirty, hairy, and uneducated. The Meiji government took away their land, language, salmon fishing, deer hunting, customs, and religion.

When Grandfather's snoring lessened, Father decided to address the subject. "Prejudice against Ainu still exists. When I finished high school, I couldn't afford to attend university. Instead, I continued to read and write. Educating myself helped me rise from janitor to foreman at the hatchery; for an Ainu, or even a half-Ainu like me, this is a significant achievement. When you and Yuri were born, we felt education spoke with the loudest voice against prejudice. Being only one-quarter Ainu, your appearances don't trigger bigotry. With your education, you will become the next generation of scientists, managers, and bosses."

The conversation switched to Yuri's experiences at the University. "I think times are changing. My roommate, Giichi, said I was no different from anyone else."

Although Akio hadn't yet experienced prejudice, he knew his family endured great hardships to provide their children with a better life. How far he could assimilate without abandoning his ancestry would be a haunting question that would stalk him throughout his life.

6. Nine Years Later

DURING THE REMAINDER OF GWEN'S CHILDHOOD, HER ANXIETY about death remained hidden beneath a protective canopy of unquestioning trust in her parents' beliefs. Her busy life at Regional High School left her no time to worry about something as far away as death. She had more pressing worries, such as applying to college during her senior year.

In the spring, Gwen awaited an answer to her applications. One Saturday morning in early April, a letter arrived postmarked from the Canada University's (CU) Department of Admissions in Vancouver. Gwen fumbled to open the letter as her mother and father paced nearby. Joining the moment's drama gave her brother, Peter, an excuse to take a break from his household chores. With a broad smile, Gwen read out loud, "Dear Ms. Sunrise, it is our pleasure to offer you. . ." Mary and Gwen embraced with feelings of happiness, love, and relief. Even her stoic father put one hand over his face trying to hide his tears of joy. Their wish had come true. Gwen was the first child in the Sunrise family's history to attend a four-year university. A university education offered the promise of a bright future for their daughter.

More happy news followed. The next letter came from the Department of Financial Assistance. Gwen's academic record, band status, and financial need granted her a generous assistance package from the Canadian government's post-secondary education funding program and the CU Aboriginal Scholarship Fund.

Throughout her freshman year, a challenging academic life, two jobs, conducting campus tours, and kayaking left Gwen no time to worry about death. During her sophomore year, as much as she loved life at CU, frightening thoughts about death stalked her like a thug in an alley. She needed advice how to avoid those alleys. Neither her mother's belief in eternal life in heaven nor her father's in an eternal spiritual existence could hide her fear of death any longer. Gwen knew she needed professional help, and asking for professional help wasn't easy. At Three Peaks she took pride in the fact she learned to solve problems on her own.

"Father," she would ask, "will you put the worm on my hook?"

"Let me show you how to do it," he would say.

He'd demonstrate the technique on his hook and continue to fish. She'd imitate him until she could do it alone.

After a screening interview, the student health service made Gwen an appointment with a clinical psychologist. On the third floor of University Hospital, a sign on an office door read, "Dr. Trisha Browning, Ph.D., Professor of Clinical Psychology." As instructed, Gwen reported to Conference Room B across the hall from her office.

Instead of the cost-saving sterility often seen in many university doctors' offices, this one resembled a smoking room in a good 'ole boys' alumni club. Three plush armchairs occupied one section of the room. Alongside each, a small end table held a box of tissues and a drinking glass. A large oak conference table dominated the room's remaining space. Gwen sat down in one of the comfortable chairs and waited.

Doctor Browning entered on time. Gwen thought Dr. Browning appeared to be in her early fifties. Her graying, long brown hair, ankle-length cotton knit skirt, and sandals suggested a reluctance to abandon her hippie days. She walked to the conference table, grabbed one of its straight back chairs, and carried it closer to Gwen. Its strategic location between her patient and the exit door allowed an unobstructed escape route in case of a hostile situation. Despite the humility of Dr. Browning's simple chair, it stood two inches higher than Gwen's, a subtlety leaving no doubt who was the alpha in the room.

"Hi, Gwendolyn," she said, "one moment, I haven't had a chance to look at your chart."

Gwen's calm exterior belied her inner nervousness. Spilling out emotions to a stranger was foreign to the culture in which she had been raised.

When the doctor finished, she formed her sentence-ending period by thrusting the pen's tip at the paper, as if throwing a dart. "Bonk, done. It helps me to write things down. Now we can start." She looked up and smiled. Her soothing tone reminded Gwen of a yoga instructor trying to relax the class. "My name is Trisha Browning. I understand Student Health referred you. Should I call you Gwendolyn?"

"Gwen or Wendy."

The doctor's first impression of Gwen was a confident young woman, comfortable meeting with an adult. Used to slouching, unkempt students, she noted Gwen sat upright in her chair with her knees held together and feet flat on the floor. She wore a clean collared blouse, skinny jeans, and flat black shoes. Her straight, black hair hung in two braids past the nape of her neck. Dr. Browning thought her looks were striking.

"Okay, Gwen, you're a second-year undergraduate. Could you tell me a little bit about yourself?"

Gwen listened and thought, *A simple question and I'm already stuck. What part of me does she want to know? How much should I reveal?*

"Gwen, are you ready?"

"Dr. Browning, I'm not sure where to start."

She nodded and wrote a note. "What's your major?"

"Biochemistry, I'm going for a B.S."

"Any future ambitions yet?" she asked.

"I'm considering scientific research or an M.D."

"Premed students complain biochemistry is their toughest course," she said, using small talk to put Gwen at ease. As the doctor asked more background questions, the more they interacted, the more comfortable Gwen felt.

"Tell me, Gwen, where in Canada did you grow up?"

"At Three Peaks First Nations Reserve on the Skeena River."

"Beautiful country. And what brings you to the clinic?"

The question took Gwen somewhat by surprise this early in the session. She expected more talk about her family, childhood, and salivating dogs. Instead, Dr. Browning went right to the heart of why Gwen had come. Gwen again questioned herself about how much information she should divulge. After an awkward silence, the doctor said, "I know talking about emotions is tough. Take your time."

"I'm afraid of death."

Dr. Browning didn't show surprise. She continued seeking clarification, "You are afraid to die?"

"No, doctor, I'm not afraid of dying. I'm afraid of not living." Saying those words brought a sense of relief to Gwen. She had never shared these feelings with anyone.

"What do you think happens when you're dead?" asked the doctor.

"I don't know."

"Is not knowing what you fear?"

"Not knowing doesn't bother me."

"Why not?"

"Not knowing leaves room for hope." Gwen knew the next question would open Pandora's box.

The doctor didn't disappoint, "Hope for what?"

Gwen felt like a child standing on a high diving board for the first time deciding whether to jump into the pool or climb back down the ladder. Knowing she had come for help, she jumped. "I hope my fears about death are wrong. I'm grasping for some glimmer of hope for an afterlife." Gwen didn't wait for her next question, "My fear is that death brings nothingness, forever; I fear life is a dream between eternities of nothingness."

"A heavy burden to carry. How long has it been?"

"I've had thoughts about the finality of death since fourth grade."

"Has religion helped you?" she asked.

Gwen told Dr. Browning about her parents' different beliefs. "I envy their beliefs in God, spirits, and an afterlife. Those beliefs shield them from the nagging anguish I feel; without them, I'm defenseless."

"Are you an atheist?"

"An atheist believes there is no God. I'm an agnostic. I don't know."

"And what happens when you have frightening thoughts?"

"Usually, I let them go. Sometimes my thoughts become fear and then outright terror. I feel trapped, powerless about not being able to do anything about death."

"What are some of your thoughts?"

Gwen began slowly choosing her words. "Sometimes I think an afterlife doesn't exist since science can't explain it. Without a body, there is no brain, no consciousness, no memory, no present, no past, no future, no self. Life is gone forever."

"When these thoughts escalate into fear and terror, what happens to you?"

Gwen described her fourth-grade panic attack. Engrossed with Gwen's story, Dr. Browning leaned forward in her chair and said, "Living with those thoughts must be frightening." She paused to reach over and fill Gwen's water glass from the pitcher on the table. "Are you okay?"

"Yes, Doctor. I was only describing what happened. I wasn't experiencing it now."

"The books say nine-years-old is young for a panic attack. I've seen a second-grader who had one."

"I hadn't had any more until this year in college."

"How has the fear of death affected your life?"

Stumped by the question, Gwen hesitated before saying, "I could use some help with the question."

"Okay, are you happy?"

"Yes, I'm happy. I love my life. I don't want to give it up." Gwen offered her therapist a tentative smile.

"How does that make you feel?" Dr. Browning continued, not satisfied with easy answers.

"Scared and conflicted," Gwen admitted. The smile receded from her face as she turned her gaze towards her hands folded in her lap.

"Conflicted?" Dr. Browning repeated.

"I want to live a productive life. If nothingness is our fate, what does it matter?" Gwen struggled to put her fears into words.

"You feel life is meaningless?" Again Dr. Browning pushed Gwen to go a little deeper.

"I feel conflicted and scared." Dr. Browning knew the answer was the best Gwen could do.

"Gwen, I see you're an intelligent young woman. We can't prevent death, but we can change your reaction to it. There is a good chance we can reduce your panic attacks and help with some of your anxiety and pain. I recommend a technique called Cognitive Behavioral Therapy, often referred to as CBT. Cognitive refers to our thoughts; behavior refers to our response to those thoughts. We'll explore how you can better respond to your thoughts. You'll learn how to prevent destructive thoughts from leading you down a spiral to panic. CBT is different from traditional analytic therapy. Most people find it more practical and oriented towards the present.

"Fear of death is a normal survival mechanism; all living things want to survive. You're suffering from a condition called thanatophobia, the exaggerated fear of death. You might benefit from being in a group with others whose problems are amenable to CBT. The process takes about ten sessions, including homework. If we have a group or can put one together, would you be willing to join?"

"Doctor, I feel comfortable with you and would prefer to continue one-on-one. I'm not ready to share my fears or feelings with anyone else, at least not for now."

"Okay, we'll continue solo for now. Your homework this week is to identify those trigger thoughts. Write them down. We'll discuss them next week. Any questions or concerns before we end today's session?"

"No, thank you," responded Gwen, feeling more comfortable and somewhat optimistic.

7. The Expo

A FEW DAYS LATER, GWEN STOPPED OUTSIDE THE SCHOOL'S cafeteria to read events posted on a bulletin board. One caught her eye:

Expo
Can Religion and Science Coexist?
Vancouver Convention Center
Friday, Saturday, Sunday
January 21, 22, 23

The polarizing topic of religion versus science piqued Gwen's interest. Without scientific proof, the afterlife many religions promised failed to give her solace. If the absence of proof no longer stood between her and being a believer, perhaps her fear of death would subside. She hoped the Expo would help. Even if it didn't, visiting the Vancouver Convention Center was always a welcome break from the classroom. One of the most popular attractions in the city, this masterpiece of environmentally sensitive architecture sits in an idyllic setting. Sometimes she would visit there just to look out over the water and watch sleek red and black freighters bob on their moorings in the water of Vancouver Harbor. She would look up across the harbor and admire the Grouse and Cypress Mountains dominating the North Vancouver skyline.

Arriving by bus after her 8:30 A.M. class, she flashed her student card at the ticket agent, allowing her entrance with a welcomed fifty percent discount. An enormous exhibition floor greeted her. Rows of individual exhibits, vendors, and food stalls filled the entire floor.

Because stopping at every exhibit couldn't be accomplished in one day, she took a scouting tour to pare her visits to those best suited to her interests. She sped by religious institutions hoping to attract new members, booths selling faith-based travel tours, energy drinks, and luggage. One exhibit pitched space-aged vegetable slicers.

Mission successful, she narrowed down her choices to a handful. The finals of the Trans-Canadian Interfaith Challenge topped her *must visit* list. She had read about Interfaith, a North American organization devoted to promoting cooperation between all faiths. Their contest challenged undergraduate students from the ten Canadian provinces to create a belief system most likely to entice someone to join. A generous scholarship awaited the victor. Over the past year, each province chose one winner to advance to the semifinals at Interfaith's headquarters in Edmonton. After that contest, only two survived to compete over three days at the Expo. The attending audience would choose a winner.

Gwen entered the designated row by passing under an arch reading "Trans-Canadian Interfaith Contest." At the check-in table, she signed an attendee list and familiarized herself with the rules. She would progress through exhibit A and exhibit B before voting. Each of the two presenters would have no more than fifteen minutes to speak, followed by a ten-minute question-and-answer period. The five minutes remaining allowed attendees to move to the next station. Since both exhibits were on the same schedule, this format allowed for a seamless progression of new audiences every half hour.

Carrying her winter coat and complimentary tote bag, Gwen walked to Exhibit A. After taking a handout sheet, she sat down on one of the ten padded folding chairs designated for the audience. Six other attendees joined her. In front of them stood two abutting tables covered by a floral, Nepalese, silk brocade tablecloth. Shoots of bamboo were roped together to form a rectangular frame looking in on the tables. A banner spelling *Naturalism* hung down from the top of the frame.

Ms. Sigrid Mattesson, a 20-year-old undergraduate art major from Nova Scotia, was Exhibit A's creator and presenter. Wearing a black yoga outfit highlighting her blonde shoulder-length hair, she sat meditating in a lotus position on top of the tables. Her eyes remained closed, her breathing slow and deep. Viewing her through the bamboo frame, Gwen felt she was looking at the painting of a Nordic goddess.

When the clock read 10:30, Sigrid's eyes opened. She slowly scanned her audience and spoke.

"A long time ago, the Incas of Peru believed a jaguar attacking the moon caused lunar eclipses. They feared, after the jaguar devoured the moon, it would descend to Earth and eat the people. Before having modern science, their solution to the problem was based on the methods passed down by their elders. They danced, shook their spears, hollered, and screamed, attempting to scare away the big cat. Beating their dogs into a howling frenzy added to the frightening noise. Each time, the moon reappeared; nobody was eaten. They believed their method worked.

"In 2001, in Nigeria, a group motivated by their religion, believed the lunar eclipse was God's punishment for a sinful nation. During an eclipse, they slaughtered all those whom they defined as sinners. In their minds, the moon's reappearance validated their actions.

"Throughout history, man has invented explanations for the unknown. Before the age of science, Greek and Roman mythology provided answers for creation, life, death, and the afterlife. Others worshiped idols. As a reward for obeying the rules established by their society, cultures promised their followers soothing answers to the unknown.

"*Naturalism* doesn't promise answers to the unknown nor does it advocate prayer. It doesn't worship a higher being, nor does it deny one exists. We don't concern ourselves with whether God created man or man created God. Our concerns are with improving observable life on earth during our time between birth and death. The existence of an afterlife is beyond our human comprehension. Why waste energy trying to answer the unanswerable?

"We live on a planet where all life flows in harmony. We're only one part of it. *Naturalism* teaches us to live in balance with the rhythms of nature. We learn to adapt ourselves to nature rather than force nature to adapt to us. We find fulfillment in life by helping all life on earth survive.

"Please look at your handout sheets. Listed is a set of values we teach: compassion, truth, charity, service, love, respect, purity, trust. They're the same attributes history has shown are necessary for any civilization to survive. Wise men taught these moral values to their followers, knowing they were antidotes to the evils causing their cultures to self-destruct. Whether those values originated from a supernatural being or not doesn't concern *Naturalism*; that they work does.

"Look what man has done in a short time. The top of the food chain is destroying itself. Raping the environment, killing each other, waging wars, and building nuclear weapons are sure formulas for man's downfall. We have a choice: fall prey to our greed or live together with each other and nature.

"Concern yourself with this life. Build a better world. Start with yourself and watch it spread. Hope to look back and congratulate yourself on a job well done. If everyone practiced

Naturalism, war and environmental suicide would end. Thank you. Do you have any questions?"

The audience for Exhibit A had grown to eight people. A professorial-looking man in his mid-sixties, well dressed in khaki pants, a blue shirt, a blue blazer, red tie, and tasseled loafers with no socks, spoke first. "Your *Naturalism* seems to contain many of the same teachings of Buddhism, Taoism, Confucianism, Bahá'í, and Shinto," he enunciated in a tone oozing with arrogance and condescension. "Aren't you concerned someone might think you've plagiarized your project?"

Having faced a year of scrutiny from her teachers and judges, Sigrid answered without hesitation, "Sir, are words such as compassion, truth, charity, service, purity, sincerity, love, and peace copyrighted? These moral teachings are part of most religions and philosophies. *Naturalism* incorporates those qualities into one faith."

The man squirmed in his chair, knowing he had no rebuttal to a twenty-year-old student. He remained silent.

An elderly couple waited for a pause in the questioning. The wife asked, "Dear, we're old now. Does your *Naturalism* offer us hope of being together after we die?"

A compassionate look came over Sigrid. She answered, "I wish I could promise you'll be together forever. *Naturalism* confines itself only to what's known. We don't deny an afterlife, but any beliefs about the unknown aren't part of our teaching."

The woman appeared angry and snapped, "Well, dear, how do you know there is no God?"

In a calm voice, Sigrid answered, "We don't say there is no God. We don't know. *Naturalism's* teachings are not dependent on the existence of God."

The woman shook her head in disagreement. She muttered to her husband, "I'm not voting for this one; I want to worship a

37

God who will take care of us forever." Her husband, who appeared to be suffering from Parkinson's dementia, remained silent.

A minute or two before the end of the question period, a lanky, twenty-year-old boy, slumped in his seat, raised his hand, and asked, "Hey, man, how can anyone stay in that lotus position for such a long time? Why don'tcha get up and stretch a little bit?"

Sigrid caught the humor, stood up to stretch and take a short walk. "Thanks, I needed that," she smiled. The young man was delighted he had caught her attention.

Gwen was impressed by the presentation. Although it incorporated much of the teachings practiced at Three Peaks, she had hoped for anything offering a hint of support for a conscious afterlife.

Gwen nodded gratefully at Sigrid before moving on to Exhibit B, *Salvation*. Looking up at the exhibit from the audience area, she saw an ornate chair decorated to resemble a large throne. Motionless on the throne sat a stoic, silent young man with the stage name of *Roland the Highest*. From his bio, Gwen read about Roland Leon Sharkansky. Roland was a theater major from Winnipeg. He was born in Brooklyn, New York, the son of Polish immigrant parents, and had been raised in Manitoba. This 21-year-old aspiring comedian and would-be actor made Gwen laugh. He was thin, rather homely, and wore a beard only on the left half of his face. On top of his head sat a white conical witch's hat with an encircling black rim. He wore a white satin robe with a black Nehru collar and oversized black buttons extending to his ankle, exposing a glimpse of his sneakers. Formal white cotton gloves covered both hands. At precisely 11 o'clock, he addressed his audience,

"I am *Roland The Highest*, himself chosen to lead Salvation here on Earth. *Salvation* is the only true faith. Our believers are the only true believers."

He paused and rose from his throne. With his large nose held proudly in the air, he scanned the audience by rotating his head 180 degrees left and right, resembling a house fan cooling the kitchen. He continued,

"And so it began. One clear, autumn night, I sat alone upon a hilltop gazing at the stars. They sent me messages from millions of light-years away. As I contemplated eternity, a vision approached me from the sky. It started as a white, flickering, pinpoint of light, enlarging as it neared. A white cloud exploded about one thousand meters above my head. The cloud condensed into the form of an old man with long white hair and a long white beard. He wore the same kind of clothes I'm wearing tonight.

"The image talked to me in a booming voice saying, 'I am the great Arft, the ruler, king, master of all. I've chosen you, Roland, to spread my word on Earth. Be ever so humble, because no man, not even you, is equal to me. I am the whole; all men are mere fractions of me. To remind you of this, only I will wear a full beard. My followers will wear a beard only on the left side of their face. I will care for you, protect you, love you, forgive you, and give meaning to your lives. In return, I demand your obedience. You must honor, cherish, and believe in me. You must practice my rituals and follow my rules. Here, Roland The Highest, take thee my *Book*. Only for those who follow it will I grant passage into the hereafter.' Arft's image dissipated into smoke, dispersing into the atmosphere."

Although Gwen found the actor's comical presentation entertaining, she wondered how he made it to the finals. She asked herself, *Why are supreme beings usually male, and what about women who choose to follow Arft? How do they grow a beard on the left side of their face?* The combination of Roland's theatrics and his robe caused him to sweat. He took a drink of water and sat back down on his throne to continue the presentation. Holding

39

up thee *Book* in his gloved right hand, he talked while poking his left index finger into its cover.

"This is thee *Book* of the beloved, gentle, nurturing, protective, loving Arft. If thee follow his rules, many of which are listed with a check mark on your handout, thou shalt reap his rewards. If thee believe in and obey the great Arft, thee will welcome death when it comes, because in death you will be granted eternal life. Picture yourself in a pristine, beautiful garden surrounded by your family and friends, crystal streams, fresh air, wine, and an endless buffet. If thou are nigh to follow Arft's rules, wrath and darkness will descend upon you, or, at best, eternal nothingness. Believeth in him, obey his demands, and thou shalt live forever."

After fifteen minutes, question time started. All hands went up.

Gwen's classmate asked, "It seems if you don't participate in rituals, you're sent to a dark place. Is it the all-loving Arft who writes your ticket?"

Roland responded, "The all-loving, all-powerful, Arft does what he does. We, mortals, obey him."

The same elderly lady from Exhibit A asked, "If my husband or I were to spend our last years with dementia, would our minds be normal again when we go to the pristine garden?"

This question first appeared to stump Roland. He hesitated before saying, "My good lady, if you believe, if you follow, if you obey, the answer is yes!" As he yelled the word, he gained confidence in his answer. He thrust his arms upward, pumped them two or three times, and yelled, "Yes, Yes, Yes!"

A wide smile came over the woman's face. She screamed, "Hallelujah, Hallelujah!" Her husband sat stone-faced in his chair, not reacting, and not seeming to comprehend. She had found the answer she wanted. "Hallelujah, Hallelujah."

Without taking the histrionics seriously, Gwen was impressed with the brilliance of *Salvation*. It replaced the frightening unknown with comforting beliefs accepted as fact by its believers.

A young woman asked, "If I don't believe in immortality, what's the purpose of believing in Arft?"

Roland acted offended by the question. "Salvation and Arft are synonymous. They're a package plan."

The same arrogant scholarly man from *Naturalism* spoke next, "I am confused," he said, with false humility. "There are so many different competing supreme beings in the world; do they fight against each other?" Figuring he had just scored a decisive blow, the professor nervously awaited the answer by tapping his tasseled loafers up and down on the floor.

Roland The Highest lived up to his lofty position; someone had asked him the same question before. "My good man, there are no other supreme beings." Checkmate, the professor lost again. Time ran out on further questions. Gwen voted for *Naturalism* and exited the contest for lunch.

As she left the food area, a salesman accosted her. He stood in front of a sign reading RELIGIOUS ITEMS. A mind-boggling array of brightly colored merchandise for all faiths filled his exhibit. Books, statues, tee shirts, pendants, brooches, bracelets, paintings, clothing, tote bags, key rings, and holy books were a few. "Come on ova' here, honey. You can't go home without something for you and the hubby," shouted the salesman, waving Gwen over to his exhibit. She thought this short, obese man wearing a plaid sports jacket and bow tie belonged in a carnival selling tickets rather than religious items at the Expo. "Take a look at these beautiful earrings, honey. You gotta believe, we gotta pair for you. You're a good-looker, try 'em on," he said, handing her a pair shaped in the form of a cross.

"They're lovely but I'm not Christian," said Gwen.

"OK, OK, I see you have a beautiful dark complexion and black hair, how about this bee-U-dee-full statue of the goddess Durga with ten arms sitting on top of a tiger?"

"I'm not Hindu," said Gwen quietly, maintaining an upright posture and a straight face.

"OK, look here at this." He held up a purple tote bag sewn with an appliqué that read—Hope For The Future.

Gwen's silence spoke volumes. She pointed at the free tote bag given to her at the entrance door. He didn't stop. He pointed at a white, porcelain night-light shaped like an angel, "Because," he said, "you look like an angel."

Having received little encouragement from Gwen, he became frustrated, "Well, what do you like to do?"

"Kayak," she responded. His sales pitch ended. Gwen thanked him and continued walking.

She next attended Dr. Rachel Smithers' keynote address concerning the topic, "Can Science and Religion Coexist?" Double doctorates in biochemistry and theology laid the groundwork for her careers as a biochemist and a Unitarian Universalist minister.

"Science and religion are compatible. Science concerns itself with the physical world; religion with the spiritual. Neither is exclusive of the other." She gave the example of Darwinism as a science compatible with religion. "Science proves the evolution of man resulted from explicable events. Religion believes those events were created by the same deity who gave man the intelligence to discover them. Conflict arises when science denies religion or religion denies science."

Addressing Gwen's concern, Dr. Smithers discussed the afterlife. "Science is concerned with our physical existence on earth. The eternal survival of a soul or spirit beyond our lives is the concern of religion. Science requires tangible proof. Religion requires a belief. While their methods might differ, the objective of both is to improve our lives." She ended her presentation by saying, "Religion and science must coexist on Earth. Why can't they both be correct?"

Gwen felt Dr. Smithers made an impassioned argument. She agreed science and religion must coexist. Nevertheless, she found beliefs not based on hard facts difficult to accept.

At the last stop on her list, fifteen individual computer stations faced a large projection screen. Above the screen hung a sign in boldface reading IMMORTALITY. Gwen watched as a scrolling cartoon portrayed the history of man's quest for immortality. The first clip dated back over forty centuries to King Gilgamesh searching for eternal life. The King learned only gods were immortal and death is man's destiny. When Gwen watched the Grim Reaper, clad in a modern running outfit, chase the King around the track, she found the humor a welcomed relief from her usual thoughts about death.

Next, a mummified Egyptian pharaoh paddled his modern kayak down a subterranean river leading from death to immortality. His boat was laden with the necessities for an eternal afterlife. Showing last before the scroll repeated, Ponce de Leon lounged poolside at a Saint Augustine, Florida nursing home. He sipped a Fountain of Youth cocktail from a glass adorned with a lime and a paper umbrella.

Still chuckling to herself, Gwen took a seat at the next available computer. Her screen read:

WELCOME TO IMMORTALITY
IS IT FOR YOU?

When a maze appeared on the computer screen, a small clock in the right upper corner started to tick away a fifteen-minute time limit. According to the instructions, the user would enter the maze on his or her first day of immortality. To continue along the path of immortality, the user had to correctly answer a series of questions. Being a teaching exercise, a liberal use of explanations offered the opportunity for the participants to change their answers.

Gwen clicked start.

Question 1:
What is your present age?

She typed in 21, and clicked, Next. A red line moved ahead through the maze.

Question 2:
Choose in what type of immortal world you want
to live?
A. You're the only one who is immortal.
B. Everyone is immortal.
C. Only selective people are immortal.

Thinking her family had to come with her, she answered C.

BUZZ—INCORRECT
RESELECT

A message appeared on the screen:

Once mortals learn about your immortality, they'll kill and dissect you to copy the secret. Mortality should be available to all people.

44

Gwen changed her choice to B.

CORRECT

The red line progressed through the maze.

Question 3:
You're now 200 years old and have retained the same physical and mental capacity you enjoyed when you were twenty-one. Before there was adequate experience, your first child received the immortality shot at age one month. She was doomed to spend eternity in a neonatal facility, unaware of her existence. Since children of immortals are born mortal, you delayed giving your second child the immortality shot until age 18. She died at age 19 in an accident. Do you want more children?
   A. Yes
   B. No

The answer was easy for her. She wanted children.

BUZZ—WARNING

The population around the world is growing to an unsustainable level. By international agreement, the birth rate may not exceed the low death rate. A worldwide blind lottery determines who will be allowed to bear children. Your odds of being selected are slim. Confirm or change your choice.

Gwen chose yes again.

ACCEPTABLE

Question 4:
I understand you still want children. At what age would you want them to receive the immortality shot?

Gwen thought since she is forever 21, having a child older than her might be awkward. She chose 20.

ACCEPTABLE

Be aware, 95% of the population chooses an age between 18 and 40. Over time, the entire world's human population will be in the same age range. A continuous influx of our youth's fresh ideas and seniors' sagacity will disappear. Thought will become stagnant.

Question 5:
You've worked at the same job for three hundred years. New ideas are rare. You want to change career paths and earn more money. Which do you prefer?
    A. High risk, high pay
    B. Low risk, low pay
    C. Stay at the same job

She chose A.

BUZZ—WARNING
RESELECT

Science can now cure or prevent most diseases. Trauma is the leading cause of death. High-risk jobs carry a high risk of traumatic death.

Neither wanting to risk traumatic death nor take a pay cut, she chose C.

CORRECT

The red path of immortality continued snaking through the maze.

Question 6:
You're now 400. You and your spouse want to go out for a night of entertainment. Your preference is:
      A. Sporting event
      B. Restaurant
      C. Theater
      D. Political Rally

She chose A.

ALL ACCEPTABLE

For each answer you should consider:
      A. Although athletes will remain young, the absence of new talent will mean you'll see the same players competing unchanged forever.
      B. As the human population continues to devastate natural resources, food is becoming a dwindling commodity. At restaurants, food is scarce and expensive.

47

C. Theater is a better choice. While actors don't age, their characters can change like chameleons with the times.

D. Attending a political rally is the best choice. Anarchy, killing, war, and chaos is looming as Earth's resources shrink. You should join any political group able to control access to remaining resources.

Question 7:
You are now 500 years old. Do you want to continue being immortal?
   A. Yes
   B. No

Gwen picked A. She moved forward along the maze.

Be aware, tedium has caused an alarming increase in suicides.

Question 8:
Now at age 2000, what path would you follow?

   A. Continue believing humans will avoid elimination from competing species, climate extremes, or depletion of natural resources.

   B. Hop a spaceship to another solar system able to support humans and reestablish a mortal human population.

She chose B.

48

With minimal death and birth rates, natural selection will end. Our species will cease to evolve. A stronger, mortal species will evolve by natural selection. Homo sapiens will lose their alpha status and become prime targets for extinction. In the unlikely event you dodged all diseases and escaped a traumatic death, hopping a spaceship to a planet with a younger sun might be your best bet. Since the immortality you seek is forever, remember, in 3.5 billion years, when the sun starts expanding into a red giant, life on earth will cease.

Congratulations, you remained immortal, for a while. HAVE A NICE LIFE!

Gwen left the exhibit despondent by what started as humor and ended with a grim picture of an immortal world she hadn't considered. Her image of immortality had been a continuum of her happy life on Earth. Despite her skepticism that now tainted her honey-coated picture of immortality, she reasoned a few thousand more years of life would offer her ample time to reassess.

The next morning she read on the online version of the Vancouver News that Roland the Highest's exhibit had won first prize. While describing her Interfaith Challenge experience to her roommate, Gwen said, "People want answers to the unknown. They believe in what they want to hear. He gave it to them."

Her roommate responded with a wink, "Maybe what Roland said is true."

8. CBT Session Two

DR. BROWNING STARTED THE SECOND SESSION WITH A QUESTION, "How went the homework?"

"Staring at trigger-thoughts in the face was difficult," said Gwen.

"I'll bet. Can you describe some of them?"

"The kind of things you might expect, cemeteries, TV murders, obituary pages, didn't bother me. They bounced off."

Dr. Browning looked up from her notes, "Why not?"

"They're not happening to me. When thoughts about death become thoughts about my death, they can lead to panic."

"Examples?"

"Last week I mentioned to you my first panic attack in fourth grade. I still remember it. The simple childhood song, 'Life is but a dream,' was the trigger. Even at age nine, I realized the dream referred to my life."

"Any more recent examples?"

"I heard a prediction about what life would be a hundred years from now. I thought about the certainty by then I'd be dead."

"How did you react?"

"My thoughts started to take me to a dark place. I pictured the nothingness of having been dead for the last three plus billion years since the Big Bang and now facing being dead again, this time forever."

"What happened then?"

"The phone rang. I forgot about it as soon as the call distracted me."

"Can you give me one more example?"

Gwen diverted her eyes downward. With a painful look, she answered, "When I was in the Aboriginal Learning Center reading a book, I saw a historical painting of thirty-eight Sioux being hung at the same time in Minnesota. The painting showed one hooded man after another on a scaffold dangling by their necks. They looked like dead chickens in a Chinatown market. I pictured myself being one of them standing there before the trap door opened. My hands and feet were tied. One hundred soldiers made escape impossible. From behind, someone rammed a hood over my head and all went dark. . . "

From the rapidity and tone of Gwen's voice, Dr. Browning sensed Gwen might lose control. She interrupted, "Gwen, let me see if I understand you. Your thoughts about death become distressing when they're associated with the inevitability of your own demise. As a scientist, you feel death may be eternal nothingness and you're powerless to do anything about it. Do I have that right?"

Gwen silently nodded yes.

Have you considered any theories that may support the existence of a conscious self beyond the grave? I know that religious and spiritual beliefs haven't worked for you.

"Yes, Dr. Browning, I think about two. In the future, science may be able to end death or find evidence for an afterlife."

Gwen knew nanotechnology, dark matter, quantum theory, black holes, fifth dimensions, unknown forces, and other galaxies were concepts now in their infancy. Perhaps someday they could prove life after death exists. She hadn't dismissed the possibility she could join in the hunt to discover the answer to immortality.

"My second hope is the 'I' factor."

"The 'I' factor?"

"Yes, the 'I,' the self, the soul. Why am I me? Why am I

51

living in this body? Why now? Why not three hundred years ago? Why aren't I a frog? Science can't explain the conscious self. A supernatural explanation may be the only answer."

"Is the possibility of conscious self-awareness persisting after death comforting to you?" asked the doctor.

"Yes, that's the hope I was talking about."

"Do you think that's possible?" asked the doctor.

"No, but I cling to the hope it is."

While they talked, Dr. Browning wrote on a flip board mounted on an easel.

"Let's put this all together."

Trigger Thoughts

1. The inevitability of your death
2. Your inability to stop it
3. Loss of all you love in life
4. Death as eternal nothingness

"You've identified these four different thoughts as triggers for panic," said Dr. Browning pointing to the list as if she was lecturing a class. "Is this a fair analysis?"

"Yes, it is."

"Let's talk about how to stop panic reactions. I recommend as soon as you've identified a trigger thought, throw it away. Picture a demon appearing on your TV screen. Change the channel and it disappears. My favorite method is to take a deep breath while changing those thoughts to something positive," the doctor said, prolonging the word positive as if collapsing an accordion. "Try out this hypothetical: a woman has a severe phobia about walking over bridges. She's terrified about crossing any bridge for fear it'll collapse. It doesn't matter how safe that bridge is. It could be the

Golden Gate or the Alex Fraser Bridge. Is her fear realistic?"

"No. It's unrealistic. Those bridges are safe."

"And if the bridge was made of rotten wooden planks held together by frayed rope and swaying 100 meters over a rocky gorge, would her fear be realistic or unrealistic?"

"So realistic I'm scared to think about it."

"If she were your friend, what would you tell her to do about crossing the safe bridge?"

This exercise reminded Gwen of happy times she had learning by playing games with her parents.

"I'd advise her to walk over the bridge with me at her side. If she became afraid, I'd help her to think about why she wanted to reach the other side; such as her favorite granddaughter was waiting there for her."

"Perfect. Let's apply that concept to you. When trigger thoughts invade your positive space, all you need to do is sweep them away. Replace them with thoughts of your work, the beach, a kayak race. With practice, you'll be able to stop trigger thoughts within seconds."

Dr. Browning checked her watch. "This has been an excellent session. You're an impressive young woman. I know talking about this subject has been difficult for you."

"Thank you."

"Your thoughts are what are causing you to have panic attacks. You can't change death but you can change your thoughts about it. Your homework this week is to practice these techniques. It's difficult and takes patience. The more you practice, the better you'll become. I want you to take control of those thoughts. Don't let them take control of you. Don't let thanatophobia steal your happy life."

9. Itsy

ABOUT TWO MONTHS LATER, GWEN CAME FACE TO FACE WITH death. On a crisp April morning, old Itsy lay on her favorite blanket next to the driveway. Had she been human, this black Labrador retriever would have been 98 years old. She had suffered for the past three years. Arthritis first set into both hips and tumors in both ears left her almost deaf. During the last two weeks, her hind legs became so weak they couldn't support the weight of her body. The poor old girl spent most nights whining in pain.

Gwen's mother and Peter took her to the vet's office in Hazleton. Dr. Sheila Barrett's conclusion was, "A spinal cord tumor is causing her hind leg weakness. An operation would be too painful an ordeal, adding nothing to Itsy's longevity or quality of life." Nobody in Gwen's family wanted to see their beloved dog suffer; nobody wanted her to die. Since Itsy was Gwen's dog, the family wanted her to decide.

On the long bus ride from Vancouver to Three Peaks, Gwen struggled with a choice between allowing her dog to continue suffering or condemning her to her own fears and nemesis — death.

While thinking about euthanasia, Gwen remembered reading about the drug, Pentothal, the veterinary drug once used to induce anesthesia during human operations. After waking up, people had no memory of the surgery. Gwen thought, *Is anesthesia a dry run for death? Is death the same nothingness as being under deep surgical anesthesia, except you never wake up? Her mind started to race. If there's an afterlife, to which species is it granted? Does conscious awareness of our imminent death only give humans a ticket to the afterlife? Ants are conscious and work in harmony with each other to find food. Do they qualify? Does Itsy qualify? Did Neanderthal's make the cut? What happens to children who die under the age of four, when they retain no memory of those years?*

Gwen had no answers for these rapid-fire questions. When nothingness became the only believable fate for all living things, she began to feel the anxiety of losing control She recognized her thoughts as triggers for a panic reaction, took two deep breaths, and pictured throwing a red ball into the river. Happy images of Itsy wagging her tail as she retrieved the ball replaced Gwen's destructive thoughts leading to panic.

By the time the bus had reached Three Peaks, Gwen had made a decision. The next day, Gwen and her family waited for Dr. Barrett's arrival. Gwen thought back to fourteen years before on her eighth birthday when she walked over to her friend Bretina's house. Gwen's birthday present was a puppy from the new litter. No doubt existed in Gwen's mind, which puppy she'd choose. Her mother always said, "The runt of the litter is the underdog." Gwen named her Itsy, short for Itsy Bitsy. The name stuck even when her dog weighed sixty pounds.

"May I hold her, Mrs. Mitchell?" Gwen asked.

"Of course, Wendy," she said, picking up the runt and putting her into Gwen's arms. Gwen fell in love for the first time. She felt overwhelmed by an intense attraction; a warm chest burn, the complete emotional and bodily surrender to the object of her affection.

Dr. Barrett arrived in her supply-ladened Jeep S.U.V. She came not with the demeanor of an executioner, but with the reverence and solemnity of a priest. Khaki pants, boots, and a plaid shirt were her standard attire. She acknowledged Mary's and Peter's presence, commented on how grown up Gwen had become, and shook Frank's hand. He had known Sheila Barrett since she was a child growing up in Three Peaks.

Peter and Gwen sat on the blanket, gently stroking Itsy. Now a fifteen-year-old high school student, Peter had become Itsy's primary caregiver and companion while his sister was away attending college. Frank stood expressionless. Mary struggled to hold back her tears.

Dr. Sheila knelt and patted Itsy on the head. Unable to lift her head off the blanket, the dog looked up with sad eyes, the pathetic look Labs give when they're staring up at you at the dinner table. "Why aren't you giving me some of your table scraps? Can't you see I'm a good dog?" The look nearly broke Gwen's heart.

The vet went to her SUV to prepare her supplies. She backed off and said, "Take your time. Let me know when you're ready."

Peter came into the kitchen, where the family waited. "Dr. Barrett wants to know if we wanted Itsy's remains buried or cremated." Father had strong feelings. He said, "At death, we should return to the earth."

Gwen went outside for one last look. Itsy lay on her blanket, calm, as if sleeping. Mary burst into tears. Peter and Gwen held theirs back. Their father's culture had taught them death is part of the Circle of Life. Like the seasons, Itsy's spirit would continue going on and on.

10. CBT Ten

GWEN ATTENDED SEVEN GROUP MEETINGS AFTER HER FIRST TWO solo sessions with Dr. Browning. They met in private for today's last session.

"How'd we do, Gwen?"

"I learned how to avoid panic attacks."

"What helped you the most?"

Gwen thought for a moment, "Changing bad thoughts into good ones."

"Can you give me an example?"

"Rather than, 'when I die, I'm never going to see my family again,' I change my thought to 'what a terrific time I spent with them last weekend.'"

"That's Cognitive Behavioral Therapy in action," Dr. Browning said, smiling as she looked at her chart. "I marked down here in my notes that during the past few group sessions, you appeared troubled by the word denial. Would you care to comment?"

"William kept telling me the answer to curing death anxiety is religion. He said, 'When I became a believer, I lost my fear of death.' I said to him, 'Beliefs aren't facts. Believing doesn't prove an afterlife exists any more than not believing proves it doesn't.' I'm afraid I offended him. He said, 'How can you deny my religious beliefs? They are facts.'"

Dr. Browning did not respond, instead she sat and waited for Gwen to continue.

"Dr. Browning, isn't rejecting thoughts contrary to his comforting beliefs just a way to deny death? Isn't sweeping away my death thoughts before they lead to a full-blown panic attack a similar form of denial?"

A slow thoughtful smile crept across Dr. Browning's face. "You're right, Gwen. CBT taught you how to prevent trigger thoughts from leading to panic. Help with your underlying fear of death belongs in other forms of therapy." Dr. Browning put her notes down. "Since we have time this afternoon, let's talk. Can you think of anything in your life which might have contributed to your thanatophobia?"

Gwen related the story about Itsy's death. "My father showed no emotion. He believes death is a continuum of life in a spiritual form. My mother's grief wasn't about Itsy's finality. She has no fear of death; she believes the living will find a better place with Jesus. Her tears were over missing our pet."

"What did you feel when Itsy died?"

Gwen paused. She wasn't used to expressing her feelings. "I don't know. I sometimes think my parents' beliefs aren't anything more than illusions shielding them from death's reality. On the other hand, I hope they're right.

Emphasizing the word *feel*, Dr. Browning repeated, "What did you *feel* when Itsy died?"

After taking a little more time to think, Gwen answered, "I felt like crying over the loss of my first love to eternal nothingness. I felt frightened my fate will be the same."

"Did you cry?"

A pained look came over Gwen's face. "No, no I didn't. I grew up imitating my father's stoicism, suppressing emotional reactions. Since I was nine, I've been conflicted about the existence of an afterlife. I feared talking about it with my parents might be taken as an insult to their beliefs."

Taking time to think about what she had said, an idea popped into Gwen's head, "Does standing naked in front of death

58

without wearing the clothes of denial, without an outlet for my emotions, have anything to do with my thanatophobia?"

"Perhaps without an outlet, internalizing your conflict has led to an exaggerated fear of death."

Dr. Browning's words hit home. Seeing Gwen's head drop, the doctor reached over, patted her on the shoulder and handed her a tissue.

Gwen nodded, "Yes, perhaps."

Dr. Browning ended the session by saying, "Come to terms with death. Accept it as an inevitable fact, and you'll be free." She offered to work with Gwen in individual counseling.

Gwen thanked Dr. Browning for her help, while thinking, *Not yet, accepting death as a natural end to life is of little comfort to me. Man eradicated smallpox. I haven't given up on eradicating death.*

11. Grad School

CBT TAUGHT GWEN HOW TO AVOID PANIC REACTIONS BUT DIDN'T alter her fear of death. During undergraduate school, her dream about discovering an answer to immortality steered her towards a major in biochemistry. In the spring before graduating, her opportunity to further pursue her goal became available. The CU School of Graduate Studies accepted her into their doctorate program in biotechnology. She hoped this choice would place her on the cutting edge of aging research.

On the first day of grad school, Dr. Ucinsky welcomed the new students, "Grad school is different; we treat you as responsible adults. While professors will guide you, success lies in your hands. The field of biotechnology is too vast for one curriculum to satisfy every student's needs. To accommodate each of your goals, we've divided the entering class into smaller groups based on similar interests."

Dr. U headed the program. Gwen had interacted with him numerous times during her undergraduate lab courses. She estimated his age to be in the mid-fifties. His khaki pants, blue dress shirt, and brown loafers matched the standard attire worn by many professors at CU. His reading glasses hung down from a strap around his skinny, runner's neck. They bounced against his chest when he walked. Gwen laughed to herself each time she saw his trademark bow tie. It brought her back to childhood when her little brother wore a squirting red polka-dot bow tie. He would unleash water on any curious child coming into range. She never shared this association with Dr. U. She figured his style was his business.

Gwen's group consisted of six students. After Dr. U's introductory talk, she met two of them. "I'm Akio Naiporo. It's my pleasure to meet you," said a young man speaking fluent English, accented with a hint of Japanese. "We're in the same group."

From the beginning, Gwen looked up to him. She had to, he was seven inches taller. Their eyes locked on each other's as they shook hands.

"I'm Gwen Sunrise. It's my pleasure to meet you."

"Gwen, isn't that short for Gwendolyn? At the University of Hokkaido, I once had an English teacher from Florida with the same name," he said.

Surprised by this handsome man's sudden appearance in front of her, she only could think to say, "Yes, it is."

He bowed and moved on to introduce himself to other students. Gwen followed him with her eyes as he walked away.

"Hello, I'm Harriet Wong."

Although they had never met, Gwen recognized Harriet from undergraduate biology classes. Often seen sitting in the front row wearing round black glasses, this studious-appearing Chinese-American woman impressed Gwen as always being happy. As they talked, Gwen asked her a question about graduate student housing.

"My husband, Richie, and I own a three-story house located near campus. It looks down the hill towards Jericho Beach. We still have one room vacant."

Gwen jumped at the opportunity to move off-campus. During a tour of the house, Gwen learned two other students also rented separate rooms on the second floor. A communal kitchen, common living room, and dining room completed the first floor. Harriet and her husband lived in a spacious basement apartment. The top floor suite remained available for paying guests.

The only rules were to lock the front door and remove your

shoes in the house. With Harriet's and Richie's help, Gwen moved in. Sharing a bathroom with June Yang was a small inconvenience.

On most days, the students prepared their own breakfasts and dinners in the shared kitchen. "May I help you find something, June?" Gwen asked when she saw June looking through drawers trying to locate a utensil to flip her fried egg.

"Yes, thank you," June answered. "I'm looking for ah ah ah ah," she said, while imitating flipping her egg with a spatula.

"Oh, yes, the spatula is in that drawer," Gwen said, pointing.

"Spat chu lah, yes, spat chu lah," June repeated to help memorize the word. Fluency was still a reach away. June had just arrived from China, where her parents and Richie's were close friends. Her real name, Jun, was now anglicized to June.

Gwen marveled at how well she did, making a dish foreign to her regular diet, in a country she had never visited, and speaking a language as far away from hers as China is from Canada.

Another housemate, tall, thin Johnny Liu, sometimes referred to by his sister as "Jumpin' Johnny," stepped in to offer June more assistance. He was a second-generation Asian-Canadian, who had been born and raised in Edmonton. He walked up beside June at the stove with hopes she would ask him for help. Petite June, wearing her floral apron and holding the spatula in readiness, gave him little more than a smile. There was no pleading request for a hero's assistance. After she flipped her egg to fry it over easy, Johnny couldn't hold back any longer. Speaking and gesticulating rapidly, Jumpin' Johnny asked, "Junie, do you want me to show ya how to crack your second egg?" I can show ya how to do it with no pieces chipping off the shell."

"Please," she said while transferring her fried egg to a plate.

"It all in the wrist, see, like this." He demonstrated his perfect technique, cracking the egg and sliding it from the shell into the hot frying pan. "See, it's all in the wrist, see!"

She smiled again, nodded her head in approval, and carried her plate to the table. Johnny stood alone, staring at the sizzling egg. While her first egg cooked, June had decided not to have a second. Now he caught on. The second egg now belonged to him.

The house's location was ideal for Gwen. A bus stopped one block away for a ten-minute ride to campus. Outside the front door, a sidewalk led down a steep hill a short walk to English Bay. The boat club, where she worked in exchange for use of their kayaks, abutted the nearby waterfront. Pelotons of cyclists, along with joggers, walkers, and baby strollers, shared the paths along the stunning peninsula. Sailboats, kayaks, canoes, and shells from nearby boat clubs sailed on beautiful English Bay. Except for a generous amount of seasonal rainfall, Vancouver's forgiving temperatures allowed for year-round outdoor activities.

As the year went on, Gwen's housemates became her family away from home. When one was down, homesick, ill, troubled, or stumped by homework, the others often came forward. Within six months, June's English had improved while Johnny fretted over his difficulty finding the girl of his dreams.

Gwen and Akio became lab partners. She called him Aki. "Aki is a girl's name," he told her. "Akio is a boy's." Aki stuck. Their similar interests in aging research had prompted Dr. Ucinsky to match them in the lab. Their academic compatibility spilled over into a close social bond. It wasn't sexual. It was more, "I'm famished. Want to go out for a snack? The Vancouver Canadians are playing baseball tonight. Interested in going? I received a call from my parents today. May I bounce something off you?"

Gwen found him smart, polite, and handsome, as did the faculty and most women. She often thought he might have a wife or girlfriend in Japan, or maybe he just wanted to be friends. She felt the same. She was here to complete her doctorate. Romance wasn't one of her priorities.

No doubt existed where his true passion lay—baseball. She had seen him pour over the statistics of the Seattle Mariners, followed all the Japanese players in the big leagues, and chatted endlessly about his idols, Ichiro Suzuki of the Mariners and Hideki Matsui of the Yankees.

One evening, Akio took the bus over to the Wong's house. He had invited Gwen, June and Johnny to a Vancouver Canadians baseball game at The Nat. The Canadians belonged to the Northwest League, a minor league team for aspiring major leaguers. "The Nat" referred to Nat Bailey Stadium.

Akio sat seven seats from the aisle followed by June, Gwen, and Johnny on his right. June's scant knowledge of baseball equaled Gwen's. "Hey, beer, getcha ice-cold beers here," yelled a potbellied vendor walking up and down the aisles. As Akio stood, raised four fingers, and started to yell to the vendor, "Four. . . ," Johnny jumped up and yelled, "Four beers here." Akio lowered his hand and remained quiet. The vendor wasted no time popping off the beer cans' aluminum tops, pouring each one into a plastic cup, and passing them down the row of fans. Johnny whipped out a fifty dollar bill and sent it down the line to the vendor, who passed change back down the line.

"Thank you, Johnny, but aren't you worried people will steal your beer and money?" asked June. Before Johnny could answer, another vendor appeared, "Hot dogs, getchure hot dogs here."

Seeing Johnny gulping his beer, Akio took the opportunity to stand up and ask, "Anyone for a hot dog or sushi from the concession stand."

The order was one hot dog for Johnny and three sushis. When the hot dog passed by June, Akio stood to squeeze his way out in front of fans seated between him and the aisle. As he moved in front of the fan next to him, the crowd stood up and hollered. With two men on base, a Vancouver player had hit a long fly ball towards the centerfield fence. A cheering fan unintentionally pushed Akio into June, spilling her beer. Quick to react, she saved the hot dog. The crowd noise quieted as fast as it had started. The center fielder had caught the ball right against the fence. That made three outs and the inning was over. Akio apologized to June and Gwen as they tried to wipe themselves dry with paper napkins. Johnny gulped his hot dog in four bites.

When Akio returned with three sushi orders and a soft drink, June was relieved to have avoided drinking the first beer of her life.

Gwen asked Akio, "What excited the crowd?" He tried to explain a fly ball, centerfield, and three outs. June and Gwen nodded without a clue to what he said.

Gwen asked Akio, "Why are you wearing your baseball glove?"

"To catch any foul ball coming our way."

"To protect us from it?" Gwen asked.

"It's more about having a souvenir."

During the eighth inning, a towering foul ball looked as if it might return to earth in their vicinity. With hopes of catching the descending ball, Akio jumped out of his seat holding his glove high above his head. Four people from the seats in front, three behind, and the hot dog passers to the left also stood with hopes of catching the same prize. As the ball honed in on the middle of this mass of reaching octopus tentacles, Akio's glove and height gave him a slight advantage. As the ball entered his glove, he pulled it against his body to thwart grasping hands.

Instead of congratulations, derision greeted this major league feat.

"Hey, that guy's got a mitt, no fair."

"You bum, you could'a hurt someone."

A 7-year-old boy with ketchup smeared on his face stood in the row in front of Akio. This little guy was wearing a VC baseball hat and sporting a kid's mitt on his left hand. He stared at the ball in Akio's glove with an expression resembling a puppy watching its master eat a steak bone. Akio took the ball out of his glove, bent down, and placed it in the little boy's mitt. Thanks and backslaps from his father, an awestruck expression on the little boy's face, and his former critics' recantations, made Akio appear as if he had cemented his place into fan history.

After nine innings, multiple explanations of outs, balls, strikes, steals, seventh-inning stretches, comparisons with a Japanese major league pitcher named Hideo Nomo, and two more orders of everything, they couldn't stop laughing.

"What's a bum? Why did they call the pitcher a bum?" asked June.

"They called you one, too," said Gwen.

"He was safe," said Johnny, trying to needle Akio.

"The ump thought he was out," Akio retorted.

"Number 18's slider dipped like a taco in salsa," Gwen added, remembering one of Akio's past descriptions. She never knew which team won but she'd always remembered the night they had at the ballpark.

A few weeks later, Gwen returned the favor. Huddled together with five racers in her boat club's launch, she and Akio motored eight kilometers from Jericho Beach to False Creek. Gwen was a member of the CU racing team competing in the national women's K-1 obstacle slalom. Similar to slalom in snow skiing, the "K" in this race stood for kayak and the "1" for the number of paddlers in the boat. While Gwen raced, Akio volunteered to watch over the team's boats at a staging area across the creek from

Granville Island.

"Number 62, Gwendolyn Sunrise from Canada University," the announcer blared through her bullhorn.

The race started from a floating platform, similar to a freestanding dock on a lake. Mounted side by side on the platform were two raised ramps resembling small water slides. A kayak balanced on top of each, ready to shoot down the six-meter slide into the water. Two contestants raced over identical parallel courses at the same time.

Gwen climbed the three steps up the ramp to where her kayak balanced. After squeezing into the cockpit, fastening the spray skirt, and adjusting her helmet, she signaled her readiness to the official. When the racer on the slide next to Gwen gave her thumbs up, the starter's air horn blasted. Both racers shifted their weights forward to propel themselves down the slide for a splashing, nose-first entry into the water. Similar to skiing around slalom poles, they paddled around colorful pylons marking the course. Before the final sprint to the finish line, each racer had to roll her kayak. With her paddle held horizontal over her head, Gwen shifted her weight to tip over her kayak. At 180 degrees, she was upside down in the water, pointing like a keel straight toward the bottom of False Creek. A coordinated twist of her pelvis and thrust of her paddle popped the kayak back to its original position. Gwen didn't understand why this maneuver was referred to as an Eskimo or Indian roll. She had never seen an Eskimo or Indian roll a kayak. Sometimes she would joke, "I may be the only Indian to ever roll a kayak."

For the first heat, the judges took each racer's best time out of two tries. As the heats progressed, racers went head to head. Gwen lost in the semifinals. A woman on the Canadian Olympic team beat her. Gwen congratulated the winner on her impressive performance.

Paddling back to the team's staging area, Gwen could see Akio taking pictures from the dock. "Terrific job, Gwen," he said, "I heard the woman who beat you won the finals."

Carrying her paddle in one arm, she acknowledged the compliment with a gentle arm squeeze. "Thanks for helping with the boats. If you're interested, maybe next week we can take out a double. I'll show you the technique."

"I'm on. Do we have to roll a kayak? That might be a bit much for my first time out."

They both laughed before Gwen reassured Akio, "We'll save the Eskimo roll for another day."

The launch dropped them off at a dock in front of the Granville Public Market. Walking through this hub of entertainment's enormous farmers' market, they passed between 50 and 100 vendors selling fresh fish, meats, vegetables, cheeses, pastries, ice cream, and crafts. Akio chose "the best sushi in Vancouver," and a beer. Gwen bought a salmon salad. They sat outside the pavilion for lunch in the sun. While they ate, Gwen said, "Aki, you don't seem quite yourself. You're so quiet. Is something bothering you?"

"I was remembering my grandfather. He recently died," he said with eyes fixed on his food.

After a long silent pause, Gwen added, "Were you close?"

"Yes, when I was little I often went with him to his work at the mushroom factory."

She listened without interrupting. "Grandfather was a link to my Ainu heritage and culture."

When he remained silent, she said, "Tell me more about him."

"It's a story he told me over years. I know he was born in northern Hokkaido in the 1920s. Some days he would talk about his hard life growing up in a traditional Ainu village where his family's survival depended on fishing and hunting. Other times he'd tell me war stories. During World War II, he fought in an Ainu unit in New Guinea. Because Ainu men tended to be larger, they were considered ferocious fighters. On the other hand, they were considered expendable. When wounded, they were usually left to die. Once he showed me a large battle scar on his left thigh. He never understood why the military gave him a ticket back home for that wound.

"After the war, prejudice was still rampant. The Japanese government considered Ainu people primitive. Assimilation offered Ainu people a pathway to survival. My grandfather married a poor Wajin woman outside of his community. Because he intermarried, his Ainu village rejected him. He and my grandmother moved to Shisaman, where he spent the rest of his life toiling in the mushroom industry."

"What's a Wajin?" Gwen asked softly, not wanting to be too intrusive into Akio's memories.

"A term for a person who is of ethnic Japanese descent."

"He was 83 when he died," Gwen said, calculating the dates.

"Yes, he died three weeks ago on June 7th, the day after the Japanese government finally recognized the Ainu as an indigenous group."

Gwen thought about the similarities between the Ainu people and her First Nations culture. "He was your link between oppressive prejudice and the opportunities you and I have today. Do you feel any guilt about the life you're living now?"

"Gwen, at what point should we Aboriginal Peoples of the world stop assimilating?

Her silent nod acknowledged she shared their common dilemma.

He continued, "Have I gone too far? Have I turned my

back on my ancestors, on my grandfather?"

"I only can tell you my situation. My parents knew First Nations children walk on a path between Native tradition and assimilation into western culture. My Irish Catholic mother and my Native father taught Peter and me the best from both cultures."

"We need a modern education to survive in the modern world, said Akio. "We can't live our lives the same as our ancestors."

Gwen was starting to feel as if she now understood Akio better. They shared the burden carried by modern Aboriginal Peoples. She felt touched by him confiding his dilemma with her. She thought this might be a perfect time to confide in him how she battled with the fear of death. She didn't know why but she couldn't share this with him, at least not yet.

"How far we're willing to assimilate is up to us. Only our hearts will tell us who we are. When you're in harmony with yourself, you'll be in harmony with your life," said Gwen.

Akio looked up and reached over to give her hand a gentle squeeze.

"Let's get some ice cream," he said. The dark cloud had lifted from his demeanor. The Akio Gwen knew was back.

12. Dissertation

DR. UCINSKY STEPPED UP TO THE PODIUM. "WELCOME TO THE Feinstein Science Auditorium. Three weeks ago our students defended their dissertations in front of our faculty's grueling scrutiny. Tomorrow, they'll receive their doctorate degrees. You'll hear them present their work today in a format understandable to an audience of friends and family. Knowing how important each family has been to you student's academic journey, I hope you'll see how your sacrifices can lead to a better world.

"Our first speaker is Gwendolyn Sunrise from Three Peaks, British Columbia. She and her lab partner, Akio Naiporo, teamed to conduct a study on aging."

Gwen took the podium. After having endured the faculty's grilling, she felt confident talking to her peers and their families.

"Professor Ucinsky, members of the faculty, classmates, guests, and families, it's my honor to present our work to you in a new format we hope is understandable to those whose dinner conversation doesn't include words such as adenosine triphosphate and free radicals.

The audience's applause and laughter set the tone for these informal presentations. Gwen hoped her effort to explain complex science would be successful. Scanning the auditorium, she saw her parents, brother, and grandmother. She wanted to reach out and thank them personally for providing her with this education.

"We've all heard people say, 'I just don't have the energy I had when I was young.' Our topic concerns the relationship between aging and our body's ability to produce energy.

"Aging has been a subject of concern to humanity throughout recorded history. An enormous breakthrough occurred in 1953. The American microbiologist James Watson and the British physicist Francis Crick discovered DNA, the basic building block of life. In 2001, mapping the human genome became a discovery as important to science as breaking the German code was for the allies to win World War II. Thanks to modern techniques, we now have a better understanding of some of the biological processes involved in aging.

"We know genes direct our bodies and minds. Like the keys on a piano, each gene plays a different sound. Which keys are playing determine the tune. When it's nighttime, genes tell us to sleep, when it's cold, they cause us to shiver. When we exercise, they direct our cells to produce more energy."

Akio sat with his family. When he looked at Gwen standing at the podium speaking eloquently, he no longer saw a friend or a lab partner. He saw an intelligent, stunning woman dressed in a dark business suit standing poised and confident.

"Our dissertation depended on three volunteer men. They're not here today, but I want to acknowledge them for helping us study the connection between energy production and aging. One of our volunteers is a healthy twenty-one-year-old, the second a healthy seventy-five-year-old, and the third a thirty-year-old with Werner's Syndrome, a rare, genetic disease causing premature aging. Signs of accelerated aging first become noticeable after puberty. Death from cancer and heart disease occurs before the age fifty. People suffering with premature aging diseases and their families are often eager to help scientists with their research aimed at finding a cure."

Gwen scanned the audience to see if people seemed engaged in her presentation. Grandmother looked content just to observe people in the audience. Except for a few trips to

Vancouver, she had spent her entire life within fifty kilometers of Three Peaks. At age fifteen, Peter appeared somewhat interested, when he was not checking out the audience for girls his age.

"An energy-producing chemical called ATP (adenosine triphosphate) is the universal provider of life's energy. It is to living organisms what gasoline is to a car. ATP is found in all forms of life, from humans to fish, to plants, to bacteria. In humans, our genes direct the steps needed to produce ATP. My research partner and I wanted to determine if there was a connection between ATP and aging. We measured ATP levels from the volunteers' cells during exercise, when more energy was needed, and during rest when the need for energy was less."

From her laptop on the table beside the podium, Gwen projected illustrations on the screen behind her of the fascinating equipment she used to measure these substances. After explaining a table of data, she summarized her findings: "We found ATP levels at rest and after exercise were far less in the older man and the man with premature aging than in the young volunteer. This finding suggested aging is related to a decreased ability to produce ATP, leading us to hypothesize perhaps ATP production plays a role in aging.

"Our next step was to determine if ATP is related to any other theory of aging. To tell us about those results, let me introduce you to my lab partner, Akio Naiporo. Akio completed his undergraduate studies at Hokkaido University in Japan, before coming to Canada University for his doctoral work in biotechnology."

Akio stepped up to the podium. "Thank you, Dr. Ucinsky and the faculty of Canada University for the privilege of studying under your guidance. And thank you to my family who traveled here from Japan to be with us today."

While the audience welcomed them, Akio's parents'

reaction delayed about fifteen-seconds while his sister, Yuri, finished translating. His mother beamed. His father held stoic. As fast as his smile struggled to emerge, it disappeared.

"The build-up of free radicals is another theory of aging. Bear with me while I try to explain. Free radicals are toxic substances that accumulate in our cells. As exhaust is a toxic byproduct of a car's energy production, free radicals are toxic substances produced by our cells' metabolism. Since our cells don't have exhaust pipes, accumulating free radicals cause them harm. The build-up of free radicals is thought to be a cause of aging. Our genes try to come to the rescue by directing chemicals to rid free radicals from our cells. Gwen and I wanted to determine if ATP is one of those helpful chemicals."

Gwen sat in the first row. She thought how impressive her lab partner looked in a business suit, a starched white shirt, and a colorful Canada University tie. His tall, athletic build reminded her of a mannequin in a men's clothing store. She admired Akio's ability to explain complex scientific concepts to a non-scientific audience.

After explaining the data from the same volunteers at rest and after exercise, Akio concluded, "The ability for cells to rid themselves of toxic free radicals was better in the young volunteer with higher ATP levels than in the two older ones. This study supported Gwen's theory of a relationship between ATP production and aging. In the future, perhaps scientists will be able to increase ATP production and help us live longer and healthier lives."

Three days after graduation, Gwen received a voice mail from Akio. "I'm leaving for Japan with my family. I'll be in touch."

Gwen closed the voice mail on her phone. She sat on her bed as the silence of the evening enveloped her. How was if possible after all the hours they had spent together that Akio could just be gone?

13. The River of No Return

FIVE YEARS PASSED SINCE GWEN DEFENDED HER DISSERTATION. To pay off school debts, car payments, and a mortgage on her condo, she was working at two jobs. Her position as a research scientist on anti-aging products with Zetheta Corporation, a large international pharmaceutical conglomerate, paid her well compared to her part-time teaching position at CU. She hadn't given up on pursuing her quest for answers to death and immortality.

Although Gwen hadn't heard from Akio in years, her close relationship with her family never changed. Almost every year from age ten, Gwen went salmon fishing with her father. This year was no different.

Three weeks ago, Gwen's Uncle Harold called his brother, Frank, from his home along the Pacific coast near Prince Rupert. "Frank, there's plenty of steelhead and coho running this year. Spawning fish are swarming the estuaries leading into the mouth of the Skeena. They're looking like a crowd of Vancouver hockey fans lined up at sunrise to buy tickets for the Stanley Cup."

Frank laughed. From their lifelong experience, both brothers knew instinct would tell the fish when the river's water level, oxygen content, and temperature offered their best chance of survival. Seasonal rains and water temperature drops often sounded the starting gun for their grueling swim upstream to spawn. Harold's reports helped Frank estimate the time fish would arrive at different sections along the Skeena.

Gwen arrived at Three Peaks on a hot night during the third week of August. Early the next morning, she and her father packed their gear into his old Ford pickup before heading northeast along the paved Kispiox Valley and Salmon River roads. When the pavement ended, they switched the truck into four-wheel drive. For long hours they bumped along service roads through forests thick with lodgepole pine and white spruce. Following the rough road running parallel to the Skeena River, they arrived at the Split River Lodge. It occupied a delta of cleared land shaped by two intersecting rivers forming the letter Y. The continuation of the Skeena veered off to the northwest while The River of No Return (RONR) split to the northeast. Guests assembled in this rustic, log lodge for warm fires, meals, wine, and plenty of fish stories. Five small log cabins heated by wood stoves stood a short walk away. On warm days, guests could be seen sitting in rocking chairs on the deck of the main lodge gazing beyond the banks of the rivers at old-growth forests and snow-capped mountains.

The Split River Lodge was a pricey destination attracting mostly affluent Canadian and American men passionate about fly fishing. Most would arrive by small charter plane and land on a dirt strip about thirty minutes away. A guide in an all-terrain vehicle would meet and transport them and their gear to the lodge.

Because Frank had spent years guiding there, the owners offered him free lodging for the weekend. "How wonderful it is to see you, Frank. Seems like you look younger every year," said Hazel.

Her husband, Ted, quipped, "And who is this gorgeous young woman with you, a model?" Not waiting for an answer, Ted continued, "I remember your little girl had the same beautiful blue eyes and shiny black braids. Wasn't she able to come this year?"

Gwen thanked him for his compliment.

After claiming their beds in an empty bunk room attached

to the main lodge, Frank and Gwen joined the others for dinner. Along with eight male guests ranging from age fifty to eighty, and two guides, Frank and Gwen joined them sitting around a long oak dinner table. The lingering sweet aroma from the morning's wood fire mixed with cedar boughs and pine resins joined the smell of venison emanating from the kitchen where Hazel prepared dinner. Ted offered the wine and fish stories while Molly, a twenty-six-year-old naturalist who worked from adventure to adventure, did everything else from serving the food to cleaning up.

"Steelhead trout are big and plentiful this year. They'll give you a fight," said Ted. "Coho, pink, and chum are here, but you'll have to look for them. Don't forget, *Catch and Release* laws apply up here."

"Is that's why we're eating venison at a fishing lodge?" one of the guests asked.

Ted smiled and nodded in response.

The next morning, Frank opted to fish the fork of the Skeena. After breakfast, he and Gwen readied their gear and walked upstream along a narrow path. The river ran on one side of the path, the forest hugged the other. Walking or canoeing were the only available modes of transportation to one of Frank's favorite fishing spots.

The colder temperatures here contrasted with Three Peaks. To ward off the chill of this late August morning, Gwen wore a skin-tight, synthetic base layer under her fleece sweater and breathable windbreaker. Both Gwen and Frank wore chest-high, neoprene fishing waders with attached boots.

At their entry point into the river, they assembled their rods, leaders, and lines. Their vests contained at least eight different pockets, each containing particular items essential for fly fishing. Around Father's neck hung his most important item: reading glasses. Standing in a river tying flies to leaders demanded sharp vision.

Before entering the water, they scouted the area. Turning over rocks and gazing into the air for insects offered hints to what the fish would be eating. They often tried to pick a fly imitating what they had found. "Take this one. It will bounce along the bottom. Hopefully, it will tempt or threaten a resting fish enough for it to strike," said Frank.

They entered the river and walked one-third the way across a mixed gravel and rock bed before stopping at an area of shallow rapids where the clear water reached mid-calf level. Frank cast first as Gwen lagged back about thirty meters to help prevent their lines from tangling. Their plan was to methodically fish their way downstream until getting a strike or reaching the lodge.

The weather turned into a postcard-perfect day. A veil of fog blanketing the river burned off with the rising sun's heat. As the day warmed, they stripped off layers of clothing.

Understanding fish behavior was in Frank Sunrise's DNA. Before becoming a guide, he had fished British Columbia's rivers with his father for as long as he could remember. He knew salmon and steelheads swam hundreds of kilometers upstream against the current. If they managed to jump over obstacles, avoid osprey, eagles, bears, raccoons, competing fish, and endure man's pollution, they often would need to rest. Any protected area in the river where the current slowed would do. Frank looked for pools of slow-moving water behind fallen trees or boulders. He knew these were inviting spots for a fish siesta.

The two waded downstream casting into as many of these areas as possible. There were no strikes until they reached a seam where turbulent, fast-moving water crashed into water moving slowly.

Gwen called out, "Father, let's cast into the seam; I've had luck in similar areas before." Frank knew salmon prefer to rest in oxygen-rich water. He was proud of how much his daughter had learned over the years.

As they approached the seam, the water level became shallow, exposing numerous medium-sized rocks with calm eddies behind them. As soon as Frank's fly entered one of the eddies, a fish struck. It put up a vigorous fight for almost ten minutes. Although Frank had changed his fly to one he thought would attract steelheads, he was surprised he had caught a male coho weighing about ten pounds.

"Sometimes luck is better than skill," he said to his daughter as he netted the fish.

"Maybe I'll catch a steelhead with a fly designed to catch a coho," said Gwen while smirking.

Frank saw his coho wore its typical spawning outfit of striking magenta sides merging with a black back. An ugly hooked nose, protruding lower jaw, enlarged head, and wasting body made him look like a witch at Halloween. Frank had seen plenty of cohos when they looked different during their ocean phase. Glistening silver scales highlighted by a blue-green back and white belly had earned them the nickname *Silver Salmon*. Frank thought if this fish could talk, it would say, "Oh, to be young again, I was once the rake of the Pacific." Age and the trials of soon-to-be fatherhood stripped this spawning coho of any hope of eternal youth. Snapping at any threat to his space, the coho looked and acted like a grumpy old man. He wore his last suit of clothes, his terminal costume. Soon, after fertilizing a female's eggs, he and she would be dead.

Frank treated the fish gently as if he were a family pet. He believed all living things are brothers and should be treated with respect. After removing the fly from its lip, he placed the fish back into the water. The gentle act of pushing the fish forward through the water moved oxygen through its gills. Each time Gwen saw a fish revived with this method, she pictured a boxer lying on his back until the count of nine, only to stagger to his feet and knock out his opponent. This fish regained its senses and darted downstream to live another day.

They continued to fish, catching and releasing two spawning female cohos and five steelheads. At the junction with the RONR (River Of No Return), they climbed from the water in time for lunch at the lodge. A siesta and hike south along the Skeena River occupied the remainder of their day.

Early the next morning after breakfast, father and daughter loaded a small, two-person ATV with gear, an ice chest, drinks, snacks, and lunch. After about three kilometers on a wide path beside the River of No Return, they reached a dead-end at a turn-around area. A laminated sign read:

Protected Spawning Area
No Fishing Beyond Here

Respecting the rules, Frank and Gwen didn't go any further. Instead, they started fishing downstream on opposite sides of the river. Gwen noticed the river's bottom had changed to a gravel bed with stones smaller than they saw on the Skeena. She knew from experience gravel too large doesn't hold eggs in place after spawning. Gravel too fine doesn't allow oxygen to reach the embryos. Her father said, "The closed area upstream has gravel beds ideal for spawning, a smart reason to close it to fishing."

Frank caught two steelheads before stopping at a natural dam stretching across a narrow section in the river. Formed by fallen logs and branches, it acted like a sieve allowing the passage of water and fish, but not fishermen. They climbed out of the river to circumvent the dam and reentered about twenty-five meters downstream. Standing in waist-deep water, Gwen cast upstream towards the base of the dam. Her first cast landed in water flowing rapidly over the top of a boulder. She suspected the calm eddy behind it was a spot fish might rest before navigating through the dam. As her fly rode the current into the eddy, the sinking-tip line dragged it along the bottom. With the power of a knock-out punch, a strike transmitted its force along her line and down the bending rod to where her index finger attempted to control the line. Roiling water near the strike zone preceded a beautiful sight when a large fish jumped about two meters out of the water before racing downstream with the current. If the strike hadn't pulled the line off Gwen's controlling finger, she would have instantly set the hook. This slight error gave the fish an advantage. The resulting slack in the line opened an opportunity for the fish to snap the line or spit out the fly.

A chess game between a human and a fish continued, a contest pitting a woman's complex brain versus a fish's instinct to survive. To Gwen's advantage, she had been on the river as long as she could remember and had learned to think like a fish. As far as she knew, fish couldn't think like a human. When she regained control of her line, the fish was still on. After Gwen released more line, her prey raced downstream until stopping in a deep pool beneath a canopy of overhanging branches. As Gwen started to reel in the slack, the added line tension caused the fish to take another short run. Gwen's lowering and raising her rod tip adjusted to this tactic. When the fish rested, she reeled in more line. After a fifteen-minute struggle, the contest was over.

Frank waded downstream with his rod in one hand and net in the other. He observed until the opportune time came to scoop this big fish into his net. They hoped keeping it submerged would increase the chances of survival.

Father looked puzzled. "This fish is unusual," he said. "It doesn't look like a steelhead. Its square tail, big teeth, and spots are typical of a coho, not a steelhead. Strange, though, I don't see any of the color changes typical of spawning."

"Maybe it's a jack coho. I've seen pictures of them spawning. Some don't show color changes," said Gwen.

Frank paused to think before saying, "Jacks are much smaller than this fish."

Because jacks leave the ocean a year earlier than normal, Frank knew they don't have time to grow to full-size.

"This fish is too large for a jack."

Gwen said, "For now maybe we could call it a super jack."

Her father felt its belly. "No eggs, must be a male coho."

This made no sense to either of them. Spawning cohos always change into their magenta spawning clothes. This one hadn't. All the others they caught and released the day before had shown unmistakable changes of aging. This one's silvery scales and normal-sized jaws appeared more like an adult coho still swimming in the ocean.

"Look at this, Gwen, no adipose fin."

Gwen knew he was referring to a small fin located on a fish's spine between its tail and large dorsal fin.

"Maybe the absence of its adipose fin is a hint," said Father.

Gwen's scientific mind kicked into fast gear. "If this is a male coho, it didn't age. Father, blood is oozing from its mouth and gills. It must have swallowed the fly. Releasing it won't accomplish anything; it won't survive. Let's put it in the cooler. I'd like to take it back to my lab in Vancouver."

Frank waited while he weighed her suggestion. "Gwen, Canada's catch and release laws don't care if a salmon is dead or alive. No matter how pointless throwing back a dead fish might seem, breaking the law can be more severe for Indigenous Peoples. I've seen how the laws can be applied differently to the detriment of our People."

While Gwen thought about her father's concern, her coho died while still in the net. Without further discussion, Father carried the fish back to the cooler in their ATV. In fifteen years of guiding, he had never seen or heard of a spawning coho retain its ocean phase appearance. He hoped Gwen could solve the mystery in her lab. Gwen hoped for the same. A fish that didn't age might contain secrets to solving the problem haunting her since fourth grade.

14. Gwen's Laboratory

GWEN FELL ASLEEP WEIGHING THE PROS AND CONS OF USING the University's lab or Zeetheta's, a choice between academia and private enterprise. Morning brought clear skies and a clearer head. She needed to think through to the pros and cons of each alternative. If both facilities gave her permission to use their labs, a private enterprise might consider any discovery their marketable property. A University would show more interest in sharing findings with the entire scientific community. Both institutions agreed to her request. Gwen chose CU.

During the drive back to Vancouver, she stopped to call her friend, Doctor Harriet Wong. They had remained close since graduate school and now shared lab space. After graduation, Harriet stayed on at CU as a full-time researcher. Harriet answered her phone and said, "I'd love to help you with this mystery fish. I must disclose, my knowledge of salmon is limited to its price per pound at the Open Air Seafood Market."

Gwen arrived at CU during the early evening on Monday, about twenty-eight hours after the catch. She enjoyed complete security clearance to enter the lab after hours. Placing his mop in the pail of water beside him, the night janitor unlocked the main door to the science building. They walked to her lab.

"Whacha got there in the cooler, Dr. Sunrise?" he asked.

"Take a look, Zach," Gwen said, opening the cover to expose her super jack coho on ice.

"Hmmm, looks like you weren't too hungry tonight. Did you order too much salmon at one of them fancy downtown restaurants?"

Zach was a fixture at CU. Now in his mid 70's, he had been on the janitorial staff for over forty years. He didn't want to retire, and the school didn't force him. Everyone who knew Zach considered him a friend. Some people in his position enjoyed intimidating new students. Not Zach, he was more of a father figure to everyone. Gwen liked him the first time she walked through the science department's door as an undergraduate.

"Hungry, Zach?" she asked.

"I like my salmon cooked, Dr. Gwen. Never cared much for sushi."

"Glad to hear it. Now I know this fish is safe. I wonder if there's a refrigerator where I can store it for a few days, somewhere between 1.5 and 3.5 degrees Celsius?"

"Hmmm, let me think. There's one in 206 B. What's in it for me?"

With a smile on her face, Gwen said, "This salmon may contain the secret to eternal youth. I'll make sure you'll be the first in line for the shot."

"I hope that shot won't make me smell like a fish, will it?"

Gwen wrapped and labeled her catch.

Property of Dr. Gwendolyn Sunrise
Department of Biology Room 318
Please Don't Touch

Given the urgency to start dissection, the next morning Dr. U permitted Gwen to begin before submitting a written project application. After taking samples from multiple organs, she attached labels and took photographs. Tissue and fluid samples were sent to various labs at CU and in Vancouver for pathological, chemical, and DNA analysis.

As work finished for the day, Harriet and Dr. Ucinsky came by to check on her progress.

"Welcome back from your fishing trip, Gwen. I didn't know you were an angler as well as a kayaker? Where did you learn how to fly fish?" asked Dr. U.

Since he went on without stopping for a response, Gwen assumed his interest in her fishing skills was rhetorical.

"And thank you for calling me about your fish," he continued while fumbling with his glasses. "Understanding why this fish escaped the rapid senescence typical of spawning Pacific salmon is a probing question. Any preliminary findings?"

Gwen started by answering his original question, "Thanks, Dr. U. I started fishing with my father as a child at Three Peaks. We take an annual fishing trip every fall. I caught this one with him yesterday. It's unusual. It appears to be a normal ocean-phase, male coho swimming in the wrong place. At this stage of development, it should have been in the ocean, not the river. He doesn't show any of the aging changes typical of spawning coho."

Dr. Ucinsky thought to himself for a few moments and asked,

"How do you know it was spawning and not just a normal fish swimming upstream?"

Gwen stopped to think. She had made the assumption a coho swimming upstream amongst thousands of spawning salmon was a spawner. She reasoned it must be abnormal since its appearance somehow defied the normal aging process. Dr. U's simple question caused her to second-guess her assumption.

"At this point, I don't have answers. I hope when data returns. . ."

"Good enough," interrupted Dr. U.

Like a continuous machine, his mind didn't stop. He wasn't being rude when he cut Gwen off. Dr. U had already anticipated what Gwen would say and offered the correct answer.

"You might want to consult the salmon lab over at the Wheeler Building. The Canadian Department of Forestry runs it. Any other findings of interest yet?" he asked.

"Yes, the adipose fin should be here between the dorsal fin and tail," Gwen said, referring to a photograph on her laptop taken earlier during the dissection. "It's missing. Based on these remnants, it had been present at one time."

With a small surgical snap, she held up a 1.1-millimeter long by 0.25-millimeter in diameter small piece of wire. "I found this embedded in the nasal cartilage."

"Any ideas, Gwen," asked Harriet, whose interest piqued. "Is it a wire splinter?"

"I looked at it under the microscope. It was etched with a line of numbers," said Gwen.

Harriet thought aloud, "Maybe it lost its fin in a fight? Maybe it ran into a sliver of wire lying on the ocean floor?"

"Stay tuned, Harriet."

Dr. U looked at his watch, "It's late. Exciting work. Keep me informed." He rushed out of the lab.

Gwen took Dr. U's advice and walked over to Wheeler Hall. At first glance, nobody seemed present in the Department of Forestry's research lab. Passing by rows of circular salmon tanks, she spotted an open door leading to a small office. A man wearing a stained lab coat sat in a swivel chair looking into his microscope. His back faced the doorway where she stood. Trying not to startle him, she tapped lightly on the door frame. No response. Her soft cough went unanswered. Gwen waited. After a long pause, he moved his head away from the microscope. Without turning around, he bellowed a loud, disapproving growl, "Whahhhht? Whaah dah yah want?"

Startled, she became defensive. She held her position in the doorway, said nothing, and waited. All of a sudden, he spun one-hundred-eighty degrees to face her. While looking through dirty glasses, his expression changed from anger to an open-mouthed, eye-popping look of surprise. Her tight, black knit sweater and skinny jeans instantly altered his mood. To enjoy the autumn air during her brief walk to Wheeler Hall, she had left her lab coat behind.

"Whoa, whahhhta we have here? My name is Peter Fogler," he said as he appeared to undress Gwen with his eyes.

Springing to his feet, he extended his right hand into a position pleading for a shake. Gwen felt as if she was a doe facing a stalking hunter. She could feel him scheming. He'd act innocent, just out for a walk in the woods, and then sneak in closer for the kill. This hunter didn't wear camouflage. Under his open lab coat, he wore a wrinkled, white shirt, and beige polyester chinos. Gwen's initial impression of this overweight man was he must be a bachelor, about thirty, who didn't iron his clothes after they'd spun in the dryer with his socks, towels, and sheets.

"Dr. Sunrise from the Department of Molecular Biology," Gwen responded, maintaining both hands by her sides.

He glanced down at his hand, extended in the air alone. As if to convince Gwen he had never offered it in the first place, he lowered it to his thigh.

"What can I dooo for you, honey?" he sang.

"I'm conducting a study about aging in spawning cohos. I heard from Dr. Ucinsky this lab has an interest in salmon."

"Your earrings are beautiful, as is your shiny, long, hair. Where are you from?" he said as if they had just met in a bar.

"I'm interested in talking to someone in your department experienced in DNA analysis of Pacific salmon. Are you the person?"

"Nah, I'm just a research assistant. The team is over at our Lake Seneca station. Director Hornsby is with them. Could I give him your address and phone number?"

A red flag went up in Gwen's mind. "I'll contact Dr. Hornsby tomorrow," she said.

Leaving Peter standing alone, Gwen turned around from her escape route in the doorway and walked back to the lab.

On the way, she reached Jake's Corner, a busy pedestrian intersection often crossed by students hurrying to class. There stood disheveled Jake, ranting through his unkempt salt and pepper beard, stained yellow by nicotine from bummed cigarettes. By night, he lived in a homeless shelter. By day, he frequented emergency departments or preached on campus at what students labeled Jake's Corner. Jake was a non-violent, functioning schizophrenic who took his medication on occasion. Today, he chose to rant doomsday sermons. Wanting to spend a little more time outside on a beautiful day, Gwen stopped to listen.

"And God made the heavens, the earth, and the water and He said, 'This is good.' He made the plants and the trees, and He said, 'This, too, is good.' He made the animals and said, 'Some of these are good, and some are bad, and the bad ones He made extinct.' Oh yes, oh yes, people. He made them extinct. He said, 'Let me make another animal with a bigger brain, with higher intelligence, one who can think beyond instinct, can reason, see into the future, imagine, and speak.' And so, He created man and hoped they would fill the world with goodness. Instead, they abused their intellect, murdered each other, and destroyed all the good He had placed upon the Earth. Hear me, people, we are the next species to become extinct. We will destroy ourselves and maybe all of God's children on Earth. Oh yes, oh yes, repent, repent, repent, now."

Noticing the discrepancy between his appearance and intelligence, Gwen felt compassion for him. She knew many schizophrenics had been highly intelligent before breaking from reality. She walked up to him and placed a Toonie into his hat. He didn't acknowledge her. He was already far away in another place. On the way back to the lab her mind turned back to Jake's sermon. She thought, *If homo sapiens become extinct, even immortal ones would die with them.*

Gwen was too busy to dwell further on Jake's words. Instead she returned to her research. She spent the rest of the day telephoning several agencies for advice. One in Vancouver, The Canadian Mark Recovery Program (CMRP), grew out of a treaty signed by the United States and Canada to share data on Pacific salmon. They suggested she pack the head and the piece of wire into a waterproof bag for delivery to the nearby Hastings Smithe Associates Environmental Laboratory.

Two weeks later, most of the results had returned. Gwen sent pages of data to Dr. U and Harriet for their review. A few days later, both came to Gwen's lab to discuss the results. Being at the end of his workday, Dr. U seemed in a relaxed mood. He checked his watch.

"Ladies, since Harriet and I have already reviewed Gwen's data, could I interest you in moving our discussion to the Peacock Pub? The beer's on me.

15. The Peacock

AFTER A SHORT WALK FROM CAMPUS, THEY REACHED THE PEACOCK Pub. Having arrived before the evening crowds expected for a Vancouver Canucks game, Dr. U, Gwen, and Harriet found a booth in a quiet corner.

The Peacock's interior resembled an old Irish pub. Sports pictures, historical beer memorabilia, and old photos of the pub adorned its dark oak walls. An expansive bar stood at the far end. The smell of beer and French fries floated in from the bar and kitchen. Customers could sit at booths, high top tables or on bar stools. As is traditional in many Irish pubs, it accommodated a mixture of people from families with children to university students and locals. The prices were reasonable, the food superb.

The present owner once told Gwen the bar still occupies the same spot where its doors opened in 1955. At that time, the street was a shady neighborhood, a different kind of shady than today. A strip parlor occupied the adjacent lot. Students who wandered in the area at night did so at their peril. Things were different now. As the university grew, the street morphed into a trendy area of gentrified condos, shops, and expensive restaurants. The word *shady* now referred to rows of magnificent hedge maples lighting up both sides of the street with their glorious yellow leaves in autumn.

Each time Gwen went to the Peacock, she remembered the time her parents and brother drove down from Three Peaks to celebrate her nineteenth birthday. Sitting at the bar in front of the taps, they ordered Gwen a tall Guinness Stout. Clive, the bartender, eyed her with suspicion. The last time he had seen

Gwen, she was underage. He asked for an ID, examined it, looked up over the tops of his glasses, and said, "Happy birthday, Gwendolyn Sunrise." Clyde prided himself on his ability to pour art forms with Guinness foam. He tipped a glass at the proper angle, straightened it when the beer reached a perfect level, and scribed a big heart on her beer's surface. Tears of happiness formed each time she thought about that evening. It reminded her of the love she had for her family, her childhood, and her life.

"How's the baby, Harriet?" asked Dr. U.

The proud mother beamed, "We're so lucky. He's two and a half now and already is on the way to being bilingual. He's in the terrific twos and shows no signs of the terrible."

"How do you manage the time? I remembered at the Christmas party last winter, your husband, Richie, told me how you take turns caring for little Daniel."

"My parents help us. They've retired and sold the laundry. Little Daniel is now the focus of their life. And you, Dr. U, what are your daughters Sarah and Heather up to now?"

Dr. U never seemed comfortable talking about himself or his family but managed to mumble, "Heather's in her last year of Vet school in Montreal and Sarah's an exchange student in Tokyo."

He steered the conversation to Gwen, "Speaking of Japan, have you heard anything from Akio? I've been trying to hook him up with Sarah while she's there."

"What a coincidence you should ask. After not hearing from him for years, out of the blue, he called me last week. I wasn't sure if he was in Japan or North America. He didn't really say much beyond that. He said he was working as a research scientist for the Japanese Fisheries Department, but didn't offer much more detail. He did talk about baseball, the Seattle Mariners, and the number of star Japanese players who came to the United States."

Beaming, Harriet asked, "Is he still single?"

Harriet adored Akio and and always delighted in encouraging Gwen to move beyond their best-of-friends relationship.

Gwen answered in a subdued voice accompanied by a shoulder shrug, "I don't know. He had to rush off before I could get his contact information. He did ask me to give you both his regards."

When the small talk became too personal, Dr. U changed the subject. Although bars aren't the usual venue for talking about complex scientific projects, Dr. U enjoyed the change of scenery.

"I had time to review the data you sent to Harriet and me. It supported our impression of your fish being a normal male coho retaining its ocean phase of development. The question remains as to why this fish showed no signs of aging or spawning. What do you think, Harriet?"

"One bit of data confused me. I have to confess, I've never heard of otoliths. What are they?"

Gwen answered, "They're calcified structures, similar to the small bones in a human ear. They help salmon with balance and coordination. As they grow, they develop patterns similar to the rings on a tree. Experts can predict a fish's life story from them, such as age, growth rate, and even diet. The effects of water temperature can leave a history of where they swam."

"I see you sent the otoliths to the Canadian Mark Recovery lab in Vancouver," said Harriet. "Amazing how they pinpointed your fish's migratory route. It started from a tributary on the upper Skeena River, swam down the river, out to the Pacific Ocean for two years, and back up the Skeena to where you caught it."

"Do you have anything from your DNA analysis?" asked Gwen

"I only found a vague irregularity on the X chromosome. Without a comparison to the normal coho genome, I don't know if it's normal or not."

Dr. U said, "I see they solved the mystery of the small wire you showed us a few weeks ago. They called it a coded wire tracker or CWT. It holds a large amount of information. I spent some time trying to understand the forty-two digit code laser-etched onto the stainless steel wire. The code told the fish's sex, dates of fertilization, and release. Even the experts couldn't identify the codes N and 1>4666."

Flipping a ball-point pen back and forth between his fingers, Dr. U looked puzzled. "I'm troubled by the observation this salmon remained in its ocean phase, despite swimming upstream with rapidly aging spawners. How did it adapt to freshwater? Why didn't it age? If not spawning, why was it there? What are your thoughts, Gwen?"

"I suspect the CWT and otolith analyses are giving us important clues. Together, they've pinpointed our fish's migratory route. We know I caught the fish on the River of No Return, a tributary of the Skeena. Since cohos return to where they were born, I suspect this one originated farther upstream from the catch site. I asked my father and the lodge owner about their experience upstream. They were unaware of any hatcheries beyond the lodge, but both admitted to never having traveled far into that area because of the prohibition of fishing there.

"I'm struck by the hatchery code 1>4666 on the CWT report. This symbol usually identifies the hatchery where a fish originates. The Canadian Bureau of Fisheries is responsible for the classification of this code. I wasn't able to find any information why its name and location are being kept secret. My opinion is our fish originated from a hatchery located somewhere upstream, perhaps on a remote section of the River of No Return?"

"What's your next step, Gwen?" asked Harriet.

"I want to return to the RONR and continue north,

beyond the catch site. Perhaps, if I can follow similar super jacks upstream, they may lead me to hatchery 1>4666."

Dr. U said, "We're a good team, but let's not tell our academic colleagues we hold our think tank meetings at the Peacock Pub. Good luck, Gwen."

Harriet concurred. Gwen felt relieved by their support. A window of only a few weeks remained before cold weather would stand in her way.

While walking home, Gwen thought back to the fourth grade when death first became personal to her. She told herself not to worry, scientists would find a path to immortality before she was too old. She now thought, *Has the time arrived? Have I stumbled onto clues leading to discovering immortality?*

16. Up the River, One

GWEN'S ADVENTURE STARTED THE NEXT WEEK. SHE FLEW FROM Vancouver to Burns Regional Airport, a half-hour drive from Three Peaks. Gazing out the plane's window, the green valleys, snaking rivers, and snow capped mountains told her she was almost home.

After having dinner and spending the night with her parents, Gwen started out on the same route taken with her father a month before. On the way out of Three Peaks, she made a stop at the reserve's food market. Besides the gear and dehydrated food purchased in Vancouver, she needed a few more supplies.

The general store abutted an open common field near the Catholic Church and the feast hall. A long wooden bench was positioned next to the main entrance. Retired tribal elders often sat there greeting and solving the issues of the day.

"Wendy Sunrise, well darn, how you've grown," said Christian Woods, a 73-year-old former soldier, carpenter, delivery man, bagger, short-order cook, and barfly. "I've known you since you were a little girl. Now, look at you, a beautiful woman. Your mother tells me you're some sort of professor down at CU."

"Hi, Chris and Big Bill, Little Bill and of course, you, Tee," Gwen responded, recognizing every one of the benchwarmers.

Chris continued, "Running away with your father's truck and kayak?"

"Just borrowing them, Chris. I'm taking a little vacation upriver to the Split River Lodge."

Sitting next to him, Little Bill, to differentiate him from Big Bill, interjected, "There's nothin' there except the Skeena and the River of No Return. Why would anyone wanna drive up there anyhow?"

Little Bill Gale, known to be a heavy smoker and heavy drinker, spoke his mind. After dropping out of school, three wives, and a lifestyle explaining his misfortunes, he had survived seventy years on the reserve. He would be the last to acknowledge this miracle had any connection to his fellow band members' kindness or the government benefits he accepted.

Gwen deadpanned her response, "I'm going up there to discover the secret to immortality."

Before anyone reacted to Gwen's answer, Tee stood up and saluted her, as if facing his commanding officer. Tee, short for Tommy Teegee, lived in a world of his own. Tee was a functional thirty-five year old who was mentally impaired from birth. His endearing simplicity made him everyone's favorite. He enjoyed dressing as a different personality each day. Today, he wore a soldier's hat and sported a toy medal pinned onto his shirt. Gwen played along. "At ease," she said, gesturing at him to sit down. He snuggled his plump body next to her.

Little Bill barked, "Why the hell, excuse my French, would anyone be looking for immortality up there? All there is are damn bears in the woods waiting to eat you."

Chris said, "Anyhow, you don't have to go up the Skeena to find immortality. It's right here." He pointed to the Catholic Church. "If you believe in the Father, the Son, and the Holy Ghost, go to church every Sunday, and keep your nose clean, you'll go to heaven and live by the side of God forever."

"Keep your nose clean, like you did?" chided Little Bill to Chris. "It's all crap. There ain't nothing waiting for you, nowhere. The white man took it all away. They took our land, our children, and everything else, then forced their damn religions and schools on us to boot. If it weren't for whitey, I'd a been something."

Silence fell over the bench, a form of communication not uncommon for people at Three Peaks. Big Bill spoke only when he had something to say. At eighty years old, Bill Gwininti stood as a pillar of the Three Peaks' First Nations band. He graduated from Regional High and earned a bachelor's degree in education at nearby River Bend Community College before earning his master's at CU. He returned home to devote his life teaching aboriginal culture, native languages, and history at Regional High School. He spent many years as the high school principal and as chief of the tribal council. Dedicating his life to keeping their customs alive, he helped the youth of their community navigate their confusing walk between two cultures.

He broke the silence, "Immortality is already here. There is no death. Time isn't a straight line. It's a circle with no beginning and no end, an eternal continuity. Your name, Sunrise, was your grandmother's name. Translated from your native language generations ago, it symbolizes rebirth in the perpetual Circle of Life: sunrise, the light of day, sunset, darkness, and sunrise once again. We never die. Our souls pass on into the spiritual world and continue to influence life on earth forever. Once we depart this life, we will walk among the spirits of our ancestors."

Gwen felt envious of his belief in an afterlife. She felt he was one of the lucky people whose spirituality, religion, or myths, provided them with answers to the unknown. It worked for them. They didn't have the fear of death that burdened her as she continued upriver in hopes of solving the mystery behind a salmon that didn't age.

She wished the men good health, shook their hands, and completed her shopping before driving to the Split River Lodge.

17. Up the River, Two

FROM THE RIVER BANK IN FRONT OF THE SPLIT RIVER LODGE, Gwen launched her kayak into the River Of No Return. She planned on being alone and out of cell contact for ten days; six days upstream, four days to return. During her teenage years, she had taken several extended wilderness trips with her father. The kayak-camping excursions she had taken with the CU Canoe and Kayak Club added to her survival skills. She felt The River of No Return's calm September water wouldn't present her with difficult technical challenges. Still, in the back of her mind lingered a worry: Why was the river which wound through the remote, uninhabited forests of British Columbia named the River of No Return? To prepare for the worst, she packed the bow and stern holds of her kayak with enough camping gear, food, and foul weather clothing to last two weeks. Her bear spray, hunting knife, and revolver added to her confidence.

The first days were delightful. Nature was her companion. Around each bend Gwen experienced the river's fickle appearance and personality changing from wide, deep, and calm to narrow, shallow, and angry. Surrounding mountains, towering pines, spruce, birches, subalpine firs, and cedars on both sides the river did the talking. Birds, deer, and an occasional bear joined the conversation. Looking high up into the mountains, she could see the white outlines of mountain goats bounding from one rock to another. An aroma of pine, cedar, and morning dew on moss replaced the city's odor of exhaust.

Being one with nature stemmed from her Indigenous values. She had learned from the writings of the great Chief Seattle:

"The earth does not belong to man, man belongs to the earth. We're part of the earth, and the earth is part of us. All animals, birds, reptiles, and insects are our brothers."

The optimistic salmon reports she had studied before the trip appeared to have been correct. She saw hundreds of salmon migrating in September's cool water, desperately trying to reach the beds where they were born. She watched their dorsal fins projecting above the surface and the spawning females using their tails to sweep holes into gravel beds. After a female deposited thousands of eggs into the hole, the fighting male's contest winner earned his place on the podium by showering the egg bed with his sperm. As Gwen had hoped, silvery super jacks could easily be seen mingling with the colorful spawners. Her plan to follow them upstream had become a reality.

Nights were routine, reminding her of camping in the back of the house during her childhood. Because she faced a greater risk of bear encounters in the wild, she stowed all food and utensils in the kayak's tight holds. Bear spray hung in a holster from her waist.

After five days on the river, the increasing number of super jacks bolstered her hopes the fish were congregating closer to their birthplace. Still, she saw no signs of a hatchery and no signs of any other human beings. At sunrise on the sixth day, when she crawled out of the tent, she spotted a mother black bear standing about twenty meters downstream with her cubs. The mother bear saw Gwen first. Although black bear attacks against humans are rare, this one hadn't read the statistics. She must have interpreted Gwen's initial sleepy steps towards her as a sign of aggression. In response, the mother bear moved out of the river to stand between her cubs and Gwen. Both held their ground. Knowing she shouldn't show fear, Gwen waved her arms, imitating a person trying to hail a cab in a downpour. With a ferocious look on her face, she wanted the bear to know who the alpha was on this block.

"Hey, bear, hey bear, hey bear," she shouted.

The bear held fast, pawed the ground, and warned of an imminent attack with pulsating, guttural, noises. Gwen removed her can of bear spray from its holster, aimed, and fired a perfect arc at the angry bear's face. The mother bear started shaking her head in response to the noxious chemical before turning towards her cubs and retreating downstream.

The threat over, and with a huge sense of relief, Gwen ate her breakfast of granola with dried fruits and nuts. She packed everything back into her kayak and continued upstream. If she didn't find where the super jacks originated by evening, this would be her last day before needing to return to the lodge. Food, supplies, work, and the possibility of deteriorating weather mandated that decision. To Gwen's great disappointment, the day ended without success.

She arose at sunrise to the sounds of water tumbling over rocks. Spawning salmon splashed as they cut through the crystal clear water. The aroma from her brewing coffee added to the euphoria of a crisp, autumn morning.

Only her thoughts tarnished nature's beauty. She couldn't help but feel her trip had been a failure. She hadn't found a hatchery or solved the super jack mystery. On a positive note, Gwen confirmed the super jack she caught with her father wasn't the only one.

After stowing her gear back into the kayak's hold and preparing to launch downstream towards the lodge, she heard the first noise in six days not belonging to nature. The whirring sounds of a helicopter came from the southwest. Tall trees on both sides of the river restricted her sky view to a narrow wedge, only enough to give her a brief glimpse of a camouflaged transport helicopter flying northeast at low altitude. Its sound reached a crescendo before passing overhead, then tapered as she lost visual contact. As the chopper continued farther away, she expected its sound to decrease. Instead, the volume remained at the same level. Less than a minute later, the noise stopped, as if it had hovered and landed.

Her mind bounced between excitement and fear. She asked herself, *Had it landed at the classified hatchery? Was the answer to the mystery fish within reach? Were clues to immortality waiting upstream?* Her plans changed. Disregarding the danger of extending her trip to the point of no return, she launched her kayak and continued paddling upstream.

18. Up the River, Three

GWEN CONTINUED TO PADDLE UPSTREAM. AFTER TWO KILOMETERS winding through a dense pine forest, the landscape changed from a masterpiece of nature to the ugliness of man's imposition. Trees suddenly disappeared. An eight-meter high cement block wall topped with barbed wire spanned across the river's width before curving out of sight on land in both directions. The River of No Return rushed towards Gwen through a large semicircular tunnel cut through its middle. The height of the tunnel allowed the torrent of water to flow through during the spring thaw. She could see sunlight shining through the other end. Guarding the entrance of the tunnel was a retractable gate made of thick vertical steel bars resembling a jail cell door. A one-meter space between each bar allowed free passage for fish and small debris, but not for kayaks. A sign attached to one of the bars read:

Tunnel Closed

Stop

Turn Back

Determined to circumvent the barrier, Gwen beached her kayak and snuggled it close to the wall. A ten-minute scouting walk along the wall's periphery revealed no opportunity for entry. Another sign attached to the wall read:

Danger

No Trespassing

Government Property

When Gwen returned to her kayak, she spotted something exciting. At least twenty-five fish rested in a calm eddy. About one-third were super jacks. She wondered, *Are these super jacks resting before they swim through the tunnel to their birthplace in Hatchery 1>4666?*

For a closer look, she waded in chest deep water along the wall up to the tunnel opening. Peering inside, she was struck by the river's turbulence as it cascaded through the tunnel. Due to resistance by the tunnel walls, the current slowed along its edges. Adding to the excitement of nearing her goal, she noticed the fourth steel bar beyond from where she stood had broken off. It left a gap in the gate slightly wider than her kayak.

Gwen knew trying to enter the tunnel through this small gap carried a risk. Capsizing in rapid water would mean being swept downstream or smacked broadside into the steel bars. She dismissed those possibilities. Nothing would stop her now. If the classified hatchery stood on the other side of this wall, she would follow the super jacks home.

After squeezing into her kayak, she attached the spray skirt. This waterproof tutu worn around her waist fit onto a rim surrounding the entire cockpit. It prevented water from entering the boat. She regretted not bringing her helmet. Having assumed the RONR wasn't considered dangerous during the fall, she figured a helmet would be unnecessary baggage.

Launching from the eddy, she paddled along the wall towards the gated tunnel. She planned to grab onto the last bar before the gap. Using it as a fulcrum, she would spin the kayak 180 degrees clockwise around the bar and pull herself through the opening. She assumed once inside, the paddling along the tunnel's edge would be easier.

Reaching the bar before the opening, Gwen grabbed onto it with her right hand. Coordinated with a weight shift, she started to spin around the bar. When the kayak pointed upstream, the rapid current smashing against the bow prevented it from turning any farther. As she pulled harder, the nose of her boat began to buffet violently against the oncoming water. Holding on any longer became impossible. She had to release her grasp on the steel bar. In a split second, the current slammed broadside into her kayak. Unable to compensate, she capsized and shot downstream, nose-first and upside-down. Being upside-down wasn't unusual for an experienced kayaker. Her fear was hitting her head on the rocks. This was no time to dwell on her helmet. Positioning the paddle over her shoulder, a flick of her hips sprung the kayak back to its normal upright position. Fortunately, she had capsized while still outside the tunnel. If she had been inside, she would have smashed into the steel bars. Instead, the powerful current swept her to safety fifty meters downstream.

While paddling back upstream in calm water hugging the riverbank, she devised a new plan. Instead of using the bar as a fulcrum, she would paddle towards the gap on a long, straight diagonal path. She hoped, by approaching at a higher speed and friendlier angle, a broadside exposure to the raging current would be avoided. Paddling at full throttle, she again neared the crashing turbulence flowing through the tunnel. Ten meters from the gap, with the nose splashing up and down against the current, she sped through the opening without touching either bar. A powerful left stroke guided her around the bar before heading toward the wall inside the tunnel. As she had predicted, the water along the tunnel's side flowed at a much slower rate. After paddling a quick five meters through the dark, dripping, moldy, tunnel, she emerged into the bright sunlight and into the unknown.

Her first glance revealed a small city surrounded by the wall. The River Of No Return bisected it from its entry inside the wall at twelve o'clock to its exit at six through the tunnel she had just navigated. Buildings clustered in the center. A transport helicopter, appearing similar to the one she had seen earlier, sat on a helipad nearby.

No sooner had Gwen pulled her kayak onto the bank, than a piercing alarm shouted its continuous blare. The security team had scrambled. Exhausted and resigned to her fate, she grabbed her water bottle and sat down on the bow of her kayak. Flashing its red and white lights, a golf cart bounced along the dirt road towards her. Three uniformed men sat inside. The driver had a look of urgency. The man in the front passenger seat held a military-style rifle aimed somewhere in Gwen's direction. In the back seat, a third man talked on his radio. Her exhausted state, compounded by these Keystone Cops and their reaction to a one hundred ten pound, dripping wet woman, ironically turned her fear into amusement. The cart screeched to a skidding halt a safe twenty-five meters away. The armed alpha male jumped out of the golf cart to assume a firing position on one knee. The driver remained behind the wheel as the back seat officer relayed a play by play description to HQ. Gwen remained sitting calmly on her kayak. She took another sip of water.

"Drop it!" commanded Rambo from one knee.

Gwen assumed "it" could only refer to one of two items: her spandex pants or her water bottle. She dropped the water bottle and awaited his next command.

"Stand up and lemme see your hands."

After straightening her long black hair, which had fallen into a mess during the capsize, she slowly stood up. Confused about which part of her hands to show, she raised them both to show she had nothing hidden in her palms. He put down his rifle and appeared more relaxed. Gwen wondered if she reminded him of a girl he might have once seen emerge from a pond during a wet tee shirt contest.

"Wahcha name?" He shouted as if she was hard of hearing.

She remained silent, hoping they'd bring her to their superior who might not consider her a lethal threat. She shook her fatiguing arms, giving a look that questioned the need to keep them elevated.

He responded, "OK, OK, put your hands down now. Wahcha your name?"

Gwen remained calm and silent. She neither answered nor changed her expression. He appeared a bit frustrated and irritated with his captive before retreating to the golf cart. Keeping his eyes on Gwen, he started to talk on his radio. This presented a dilemma for the driver. Rambo stood between him and his view of Gwen. Instead of a ferocious and dangerous invader, all the driver saw was a beautiful young woman in spandex pants and a soaked tee-shirt. Extending his shoulders and neck outside the cart solved his problem of seeing around Rambo.

"Callahan to base, Callahan to base." Rambo called into a handheld radio.

Gwen noticed the three guys looked sharp. Their clean khaki uniforms sported the Department of Fisheries and Oceans' patch on the right upper arm and SECURITY on the chest. Their last names were sewn underneath.

"Deveaux at base. Go ahead, Callahan."

"We gotta dumb injun here who crashed the tunnel in a kayak. She don't talk. She don't do nothin' 'cept stand there and look dumb."

"OK, Callahan, bring her in," Deveaux said.

"Should I cuff 'er, Cap?"

"No."

The siren stopped coincident with Peters in the back seat turning off his radio. Peters signaled Gwen to sit in Callahan's former position in the front. They didn't talk to her, only gestured.

She guessed they figured if she didn't speak, she couldn't hear either. Callahan now sat behind her. From there, he could react in case she jumped out of the cart and tried to escape by climbing barefoot over the towering wall, cut the barbed wire with her bare hands, and fled into the solitude of the vast northwest forest.

After a short drive, they arrived at a metal door on the ground floor of the central building. The door sign read:

SECURITY.

Using fingerprint recognition, Callahan opened the door and flicked his head up to signal Gwen to enter.

"Here she is, Captain."

In a modest office, behind a small desk, sat a well-groomed man in his late thirties. He wore the same uniform as Callahan. His shirt read, Captain Deveaux, Chief of Security. He was writing when they entered. When he looked up, he did an actual double-take. He put the pen down beside a framed photograph of his wife and three small children before pointing to the chair in front of his desk.

"Please have a seat, Miss."

"Need me to stay, sir?"

"No, that will be all, Callahan."

Waiting until Gwen sat, Deveaux pointed to one of the security monitors on the wall. His finger stopped at one showing a live image of the tunnel's barred gate.

"You did an impressive piece of kayaking. I worried when you capsized on your first try. We once had some swimmers make it through, never a kayak or canoe. The broken bar has been on order now for over two months. Welcome to the government.

"May I have your name, please?"

"Yes, sir, it's Doctor Gwendolyn Sunrise."

"G-w-e-n-d-o-l-y-n?" He spelled it out as he wrote it down. "Correct."

"A doctor," he said, nodding his head up and down with approval. "And what brings you here?"

Gwen explained to him her position at CU, the entire story of the super jack, and its possible connection to her aging research. He seemed enthralled with the story.

"And why would you commit a crime on government property to obtain such information?"

She thought for a few moments. "Captain, the quest for scientific knowledge is an uncontrollable urge for me, like chocolate is for others. Sometimes, you have to take a chance."

He smiled and picked up the phone.

"Is that you, doctor? It's Claude. Oh, yes, I'm just fine. Oh, I heard all right. Seven to five. Big win, Doc. I have an unexpected visitor here who has some questions. I thought you might be able to help her. Do you have time? Now? Sure thing; I'll be right up."

19. Hatchery 1>4666

"Doctor Sunrise, I've arranged for you to meet one of our researchers," said Captain DeVeaux. "Anything you need first?"

"My clothes and cell phone are in the kayak's front hold. The guards will find a handgun, hunting knife, and bear spray in there too."

"I'll have Callahan do it. The cell phone and weapons need to wait until Ottawa gives us clearance."

They walked up a flight of stairs and down a long hallway inside the main research building. After passing many offices and labs, they stopped at one with *Canadian Joint Fisheries Study Project* etched onto the door's frosted glass. The moment Gwen entered the room, her life changed.

"Dr. Naiporo, please meet Dr. Gwendolyn Sunrise, an unexpected visitor from Canada University. She's interested in Pacific salmon and aging. Dr. Sunrise, meet Dr. Akio Naiporo, director of the Japanese division of our Joint Fisheries Project."

Their eyes fixed on each other like magnets. Her heart raced. She wanted to jump into his arms and hold him. Only a greater force and an unspoken need to act like strangers held them apart.

"I'm pleased to meet you, Dr. Sunrise," he said, extending his hand.

Following the script indicated by his formality, she shook his hand.

"Pleased to meet you, Dr. Naiporo."

As Captain Deveaux opened the door to leave, he turned towards Akio, winked, and said, "Seven to five, Doc, how about

110

those Jays!"

Gwen thought, *I should have known. They're baseball buddies.*

So many questions swirled in her head: *Would I be charged with a crime? How would I paddle back without more supplies? How cold would it be? What secrets do the super jacks hold? Why hadn't Akio told me he worked here? Why a fort? Why the secrecy? Why are the governments of Japan and Canada involved?*

Akio led Gwen to his small, unmonitored office off the lab and closed the door. When they turned towards each other, it was as if two magnets came together. They snapped into each other's arms, embracing with a feeling never present during all the platonic hugs they shared in graduate school.

He stepped backward and smiled, shaking his head in disbelief.

"Well, look at you," he said with a gesture meaning, "What are you doing here?"

Gwen was flooded with memories. *We never had trouble communicating. So many dinners, so many outings, so many hours working in the lab; we never ran out of things to say.*

Gwen filled Akio in on the fishing trip with her father, the super jack, her research, the CWT, and the helicopter. She had questions for Akio as well. As she was about to ask him why he never told her he was in the country, Michiko Takahashi, his technician from Japan, knocked on the door. She delivered Gwen's personal items and cell phone. Akio asked Michiko to help Dr. Sunrise find the shower and changing facility.

Being clean and dry provided Gwen with a welcome relief. Miki, as the assistant asked to be called, led Gwen back to Akio's office. He suggested a tour might be the best way to answer her questions, adding a promise to include lunch.

They exited the lab and climbed two flights of stairs

leading to a large observation deck on the research building's roof. Pointing down the river towards the tunnel, Gwen said, "See my transportation. Does it bring back memories of the kayak races I dragged you to in Vancouver?"

Akio nodded and gave Gwen a warm affectionate smile, "Of course I remember. You had a great race. Talking about kayaking, how did you maneuver through the gate?"

Gwen gave him the details of her adventure. His grin and subtle shaking of his head told her he wasn't surprised. From other locations on the roof, she saw the wall forming an oval barrier around the entire complex. Beyond it, densely forested hills and distant glacier-capped mountains covered the landscape. Except for a small patch devoted to sustainable farming, the rest of the interior to the west of the river lay barren.

Akio pointed towards the east and said, "Take a look at those two windowless buildings, the ones surrounded by a separate fence. See them, over there, next to the fire station, warehouses, garages, communication tower, and dormitories?"

"The ones guarded by soldiers?

"Yes, with military vehicles lining the periphery. Look next to it. Is that the helicopter you saw this morning?"

"It looks similar. When it flew over, I only caught a glimpse of it through the trees. I see soldiers are now unloading its cargo. What's going on there? Some of the boxes are labeled "Explosive?"

Akio let the question hang unanswered as they walked downstairs to a smaller observation deck looking at the river flowing over a low dam. A fish ladder branched off the building-side of the river.

"This is the hatchery area where we release and collect the salmon in our project."

Gwen had difficulty paying attention to his tour. The last she saw Akio was five years ago at graduation. He left with his family for Japan a few days after the ceremony. She couldn't stop thinking about the four years they spent together. Now, at thirty-five, he still maintained his athletic build. His new role as a director of the Japanese section hadn't changed his boyish charm. She wanted to hold him. How long had he been here and why hadn't he called?

They walked down more flights to the underground level. Two glass panels allowed researchers to view fish as they either continued upstream past the dam or were diverted into a holding tank. Gwen watched as one super jack swam into the tank.

"What do you think, Dr. Sunrise?" Akio asked. His ear-to-ear grin told her he might have contributed to its design. She acknowledged the setup with an approving smile. He said, "The Canada Department of Fisheries and Oceans launched this international project to study the declining Pacific salmon population."

He described how a declining salmon population was a problem affecting the entire Pacific Rim. All bordering countries received applications for the opportunity to work on the problem with the Canadians. The Japanese Ministry of Agriculture, Forestry and Fisheries had expressed an interest. They handed the application process to a respected scientist, Dr. Nabuo Murakami, chief of the Division of In Vitro Fertilization at the Imperial Institute of Genetics in Tokyo. His impeccable scientific reputation, credentials, and research experience landed him the job.

Akio explained how Hokkaido was surrounded by the Pacific Ocean, the Sea of Japan, and the Sea of Okhotsk. Their rivers historically provided fertile spawning grounds for Pacific salmon. Working in salmon hatcheries his entire adult life, Akio's father had witnessed the decline of returning salmon due to the ill effects man-made obstacles and pollution had on their natural life cycle. When the voracious appetite for salmon among the Japanese people and the income garnered from the salmon industry suffered, the Japanese government listened.

"Dr. Murakami wrote an irresistible project which gained Japan's acceptance into the study. It concerned the puzzling question of what draws salmon back to their birthplace to spawn."

Akio outlined for Gwen how the plan worked. He described how the eggs and sperm harvested from cohos returning to spawn in Hokkaido rivers were fertilized in a Japanese laboratory.

"The new embryos were flown to me in Canada, where we incubated and grew them in our hatchery tanks. One and one-half years later, we injected a CWT or Coded Wire Tracker into each fish's snout."

He continued describing how they clipped the adipose fin before releasing a fish into the RONR where they remained for about one year before entering the ocean for two to three more.

"My team studied them when they returned to the RONR to spawn. If their Japanese genetic make-up directed those salmon, they would return to Japan. If guided by their environment, they would return to Canada," explained Akio.

"Excellent study. I see why the Canadians accepted it."

"Since our study has ended, let me walk you through the steps we took when returning fish were plentiful." Akio turned and introduced Gwen to a technician sitting at a control panel in front of the viewing windows.

"Gwen, this is my colleague, Hannah. Hannah, meet Gwen Sunrise, a visiting doctor." A small Asian woman, Hannah stood, smiled, and shook Gwen's hand before returning to her seat near the observation window.

"Hannah can open and close gates to direct fish from the ladder into that holding tank or allow them to continue swimming upstream." Akio pointed to an area in the water beyond the viewing glass. "Suppose a project coho, identified by a missing adipose fin, swam up the ladder. She would divert it into the holding tank. Other technicians would remove those fish to scan their snouts with a CWT reading wand. The information went to a computer's database, where a technician could add miscellaneous comments. For instance, someone would enter the code word *Lamda* for each coho you call a super jack. All data was transmitted to the project's parent organizations in Ottawa, Tokyo, and Hokkaido. Most fish were out of water for less than thirty-seconds before being released upstream."

Gwen listened to every word. She was fascinated. The missing adipose fin and CWT wire now made sense. She decided to wait for Akio to say more about the super jacks or *Lamdas*.

Instead he asked, "Interested in lunch?"

"Ravenous."

The dining area reminded Gwen of a smaller version of their cafeteria at CU. You pick up your tray, push it along a chrome slide, and serve yourself. After seven days on the river, Gwen wasn't complaining.

Akio introduced her to one of his colleagues, "Dr. Sunrise, meet Dr. Kenneth Rosenstat, director of the project's Canadian division. Gwen is from CU. She is interested in the rapid senescence of Pacific salmon."

"I heard from Captain DeVeaux you caught one of our *Lamdas* on a fishing vacation. We're also trying to determine why it didn't age," said Dr. Rosenstat. Although Dr. Rosenstat was polite, he didn't offer Gwen any insight into *Lamda*.

They exchanged pleasantries before he went back to his table.

"Questions so far?" Akio asked.

After eating dehydrated camping food for a week, the

amount of food Gwen devoured prevented a quick answer. Two or three swallows later, she said, "I noticed your lab had several of the same instruments we used at CU during our ATP research. A coincidence?"

"No coincidence. Our project director in Tokyo, Dr. Murakami, added an ATP section to the study soon after hiring me. Maybe he had read our dissertation. I'm not sure. I do know he has a side interest in aging research."

"Why was he interested in a salmon project?"

"The interest didn't start with him. It started with the Japanese government. Dwindling numbers of cohos returning to Japanese rivers had a negative financial impact on Japan. Since Canada's return rate for coho was far larger than Japan's, the Japanese Department of Agriculture, Forestry and Fisheries felt they might be able to learn from Canada more about how to increase the return of Pacific coho to Japanese water. They hired Murakami to write the application. I do know he used coho salmon in his aging research but I doubt he had prior knowledge of this project."

"How did you become involved?"

"After Canada accepted Japan's application, Japan appointed Dr. Murakami to direct the entire Japanese project. He needed a research scientist to head the operation overseas in Canada and wanted a Ph.D. interested in aging research, fluent in English, and familiar with Canada. I matched his criteria. The generous salary matched mine."

"Any results yet?" Gwen asked.

"The ATP study is complete. As we reported in our dissertation on ATP in humans, ATP levels fell in aging salmon."

"I would have predicted ATP levels would rise in salmon needing extra energy to swim from the ocean to their spawning grounds," said Gwen.

"I would have thought the same. It appears the aging process trumps the need for generating more energy."

"Any results yet on the main study?"

Akio didn't answer. He looked around at the tables filled with people sitting nearby.

"Let's walk back into my office. We can talk more there."

With the office door closed, Akio felt more relaxed. There were no cameras in his office.

"The project was either a success or a disaster."

"What part was the success?" asked Gwen.

"As planned, two days after being fertilized at GenLab in Hokkaido, the coho eggs arrived here. We incubated and raised them using standard hatchery methods. When they reached eighteen months, we released them into the river. After spending a year in the River of No Return and the Skeena, they reached the Pacific for two or three more years in the ocean. When the spawning fish reentered the Skeena, they started to return here. We knew the Japanese were on the lookout for our project fish returning to their rivers. They reported none were found."

Gwen said, "I understand. Where the fish were born and raised, rather than their Japanese genes, dictated where they would return. That part of your study sounds successful. What part is the disaster?"

"Time will tell, but we're worried the *Lamdas* have the potential to cause large problems. A significant number of the returning males have been *Lamdas*. All returning project females appeared to be normal spawners."

"Aki, you always were unflappable. You seem concerned about the *Lamdas*. Tell me what you're thinking."

"The Canadians and I are concerned about *Lamdas* dominating the entire native population."

"What's been done to prevent it?"

117

"About two months ago, we caught and destroyed all returning *Lamdas*. It's been a case of too little, too late. At least a month went by before we discovered the problem. The fish ladder had been wide open part of every day and all night. No doubt *Lamdas* migrated upstream."

Gwen nodded her head as she contemplated the implication *Lamda* might have on the wild salmon population. A fish that didn't age could dominate the entire species. After a short pause she asked, "There's something else I couldn't figure out. Whats the significance of the two unknown codes on the CWT wire? What is the code N, and why is the hatchery code designated as 1>4666 classified?"

"The wire markers came to us from Japan in thirty spools. Except for the same confusion you had about those two codes, we found the CWTs in order."

"What do they mean?"

"The Canadians asked for the hatchery code to be classified. They reasoned a research facility shouldn't be designated a hatchery or coded as one. The N is a mark the Japanese use to indicate the fish originated from eggs fertilized in Japan, Akio explained."

"Sounds logical. Another question, I don't understand the amount of security and secrecy here. I can't decide if this is a research facility or a military fort."

Before Akio could address Gwen's question, his phone rang.

"Akio here. Ken? Yes, we're just about ending the tour. Yes, of course, she's aware of *Lamda*. Her findings were identical to ours. Tomorrow morning? Yes, Ken, I understand. I'm worried, too. I'll make arrangements. Thank you, good-bye."

Akio's silent pause, followed by a sigh, told Gwen what she suspected. The project considered a mutation as a possible

118

cause of *Lamda.*

"Aki, I think a mutation might have caused *Lamda,* perhaps during the fertilization process."

"Ken and I are also worried. If *Lamda* breeds or cross-breeds, the resulting progeny could play havoc with an already fragile natural balance of salmon in the entire Pacific Rim."

Gwen added, "I've read about invasive fish. Without natural predators, they have the potential to disrupt entire aquatic ecosystems." Her concern about *Lamda's* potential to harm the entire Pacific salmon population conflicted with her excitement over a mutation related to the aging process.

On a brighter note, Ken instructed Akio to leave for Japan as soon as possible. Ottawa felt Akio's superiors in Japan might be able to shed light on *Lamda.* The Canadians offered Gwen, along with her father's kayak, to ride on the helicopter with Akio back to Vancouver. Captain DeVeaux had forgiven her trespassing.

"The situation is serious, Gwen."

Reading into his tone, Gwen answered what she thought he meant, "I won't mention this facility to anyone else."

He nodded approval as he stood up from behind his desk. She did the same from her chair. They paused, looked at each other, and embraced for what seemed to her forever.

At 7 A.M., the next morning, they left on the helicopter with other employees and soldiers. En route to Vancouver, Gwen caught a glimpse of Three Peaks and thought about her childhood's blissful simplicity.

Akio's flight to Tokyo didn't leave until the next day. They walked around the campus, stopped by the Peacock, and visited the Granville Public Market. Walking back to her condo from the market, Gwen asked again why the project hatchery resembled a fort rather than a research facility. She described the thick perimeter wall, a gated tunnel, barbed wire barriers, and armed soldiers.

Akio answered, "Even the Canadian team doesn't seem to know the answer. It's a don't ask, don't tell situation. I doubt the perimeter wall and gated tunnels were constructed to prevent wild First Nations women from stealing our salmon. I suspect this facility was built as a secret underground bunker headquarters for governmental leaders during a national emergency. Our project may provide cover for their primary intention."

Gwen invited Akio to stay over at her condo. He did. Their relationship climbed to a different level.

20. GenLife

WHILE GWEN SETTLED BACK TO LIFE IN VANCOUVER, AKIO LEFT the next afternoon on a flight to Sapporo. A connection in Tokyo and a sixteen-hour time zone change left him exhausted. After a night recovering at his parents' condo, he devoted the next day to business.

His first stop at the Pan Japanese Fisheries Agency in Hokkaido reunited him with his colleague, Dr. Hideo Nichibori. Being young Japanese men raised to honor tradition, they first exchanged bows before slapping each other on the backs and fist-pumping.

"Akio, my friend, I'm glad to see you in person after years of emails and phone calls from Canada."

"Nich, it feels like yesterday when we worked here together."

Fresh out of graduate school, Akio took his first job at Pan Fisheries, where Dr. Nichibori was the director. Both young scientists bonded over work and sports. Akio gave him his nickname, "Nich."

During that time, Japan joined the Canadian Joint Fisheries Research Project. The head of the Japanese section, Dr. Nabuo Murakami, made the decision to stage the project from Hokkaido, rather than in Tokyo. He had his reasons. Since most Japanese salmon returned to Hokkaido rivers, Pan Fisheries was the logical choice. Dr. Murakami chose Dr. Nichibori to direct clinical operations from Japan. As clinical chief of the project in Canada, Akio answered to Nich and Nich answered to Murakami.

After reminiscing about their times together, they sat

down at a small conference table covered with pages of data from Canada.

With his business face on, Nich said, "Akio, I recalled you from Canada to talk about *Lamda*. Director Murakami is well aware of it. After feeling the heat coming from Ottawa, he relegated the entire problem to me."

Nich's raised eyebrows, along with a subtle negative shake of his head, expressed his feelings about the director.

After they analyzed data, Nich explained his theory about *Lamda*. Pointing at columns of numbers, he said, "I see a numerical relationship giving us an important clue to solving the *Lamda* mystery. All the *Lamdas* returning to the hatchery were male cohos belonging to the project. All returning project females appeared to be normal, spawning cohos. Those statistics point to a sex-linked trait, in this case, a mutation on the egg's X chromosome."

The simplicity of his theory embarrassed Akio. "I feel as if I just found my lost sunglasses sitting on top of my baseball hat. Those numbers had been in front of me for almost a year."

Akio was well aware a sex-linked trait is one carried by genes on chromosomes determining sex. He knew males possess an X and a Y chromosome and females carry two X's. Traits caused by genes on those chromosomes are predictable, similar to flipping a coin, rolling dice, or the fifty-fifty split between males and females. Akio thought out loud to ensure he understood Nich's theory.

"Nich, since each egg contains only one X chromosome, if the mutation causing *Lamda* occurred on the X chromosome carried in eggs fertilized at GenLife, only male XY offspring would exhibit the *Lamda* trait. The XX females with one mutated X chromosome would appear normal. Both X's need to be mutated for the trait to show in females. That's what we observed in Canada.

All the *Lamdas* were males. All the females appeared normal."

Nich sat with his forearm relaxed on the table, tapping his pencil up and down. With a proud smirk on his face, he nodded in agreement. Akio shook his head in disbelief, slapped his forehead, and said, "Of course you're right, it's so obvious, where was I?"

Now their investigation had direction. Jumping ahead to discuss the possibilities of what could have caused the mutation, they narrowed down the choices to two: a mutation caused by steps in fertilization or genetic manipulation by humans.

After a thirty minute drive, they arrived at the hatchery where the project's eggs and sperm originated.

"Dr. Naiporo, please meet Mr. Yoshio Fukahori, the manager of the South Hokkaido Fish Hatchery," said Nich.

After exchanging business cards, Mr. Fukahori showed a poster outlining the steps taken on the day the eggs and sperm were harvested from spawning coho salmon and trucked straight to GenLife for fertilization.

"We don't have fish today, but Dr. Nichibori observed us that day. He saw the eggs harvested and pooled together into these sterile stainless steel vats containing unprocessed river water. The sperm went through the same process before being transported in separate containers to GenLife."

Akio and Nich checked the hatchery's books to confirm the timing and methodology. Both noted several other similar deliveries to GenLife had occurred earlier in the year.

"Were you given any reason why GenLife needed so many deliveries?" asked Nich.

Fukahori said, "I'm afraid I don't know. Perhaps you should talk to Dr. Okawa at GenLife."

Keeping that in mind, the two young scientists were satisfied no other irregularities occurred at the hatchery. On the drive to GenLife, Akio asked Nich, "Who is in charge of the lab at GenLife?"

"Dr. Masahiko Okawa."

"The same Dr. Okawa who finished runner-up for a Nobel Prize in Medicine?"

"Yes, the same one who directed the In Vitro Fertilization Department at the Imperial Institute of Genetics in Tokyo before Dr. Murakami took over."

"I didn't know Dr. Okawa is now working in a private lab. Do you know why he left the Institute of Genetics?"

"He told me he wanted to offer the benefits of his experience directly to the people."

"You've met him?"

"Several times, about this project—all positive experiences. He was the brains behind fertilizing the eggs and sending them to you in Canada."

"How did Murakami persuade him to join the project?"

"Murakami was his protege. When Dr. Okawa retired from the Imperial Institute in 2005, Murakami took over his position and Okawa moved to Hokkaido to start GenLife."

They drove into GenLife's parking lot. The lab occupied a modern building situated on meticulously landscaped grounds. A glass main entrance door welcomed them into a large reception area. The decor looked to Akio more like a posh hotel lobby rather than a laboratory. Beautiful paintings depicting traditional Japanese landscapes and history adorned the walls.

GenLife worked on the cutting edge of egg, sperm, and embryo technology. It deserved its reputation for excellence and discretion. Offering a wide variety of sensitive services, including prenatal testing for over forty human genetic disorders, GenLife helped women and their families make informed decisions.

A receptionist escorted Akio and Nich to Doctor Okawa's office. Sitting at his desk, the doctor appeared to be in his early seventies. His long white lab coat, gray mustache, round glasses, and calm expression reminded Akio of someone's venerable grandfather. Dominating the wall behind his desk hung a painting of particular beauty. The sun goddess, Amaterasu, draped in a gold silk gown emerged from the earth with her eyes focused toward the sky. On her head sat a jewel-studded crown, radiating golden beams toward the heavens.

Showing respect for Dr. Okawa, Nich and Akio bowed deeply in unison. Dr. Okawa stood up, bowed, and circled his desk to greet Nichibori by name. Nich introduced him to Dr. Naiporo.

Dr. Okawa preempted any of their prepared questions by opening the conversation.

"Gentlemen, I've been following your project, fascinating work. I've always wondered how salmon find their way back to their original spawning grounds. I'm aware of the *Lamda* problem. What are your thoughts?"

Nich showed him their data supporting a sex-link mutation. Dr. Okawa listened, stroked his chin, and waited until Nich finished. "When we process ova and sperm in human IVF, mutations are rare but can happen. Your theory of a sex-linked mutation is possible. Working with salmon has been a new adventure for me. When I joined your project, I had much to learn. Developing effective techniques took me through many failed trials. I had to use several batches of eggs and sperm from the hatchery before I was able to succeed."

Nich and Akio glanced at each with a gesture indicating Dr. Okawa had answered their concern. He had needed several deliveries from the hatchery to help him develop an effective technique. No red flags there."

Dr. Okawa continued, "I studied some of Lamda's genes. In support of your theory, I saw an irregularity on the X chromosome. Without a coho gene map, I don't know if it's normal or not. As you know, the coho salmon genome hasn't yet been mapped. "

Nich asked, "Are you aware of any ongoing coho genome projects?"

"Dr. Murakami's department in Tokyo now has researchers mapping the entire genome," answered Dr. Okawa.

Neither Niche nor Akio were aware of Murakami's genome project. They both sat stoically trying not to show any emotional reaction to the shock they were feeling over Dr. Okawa's revelation. They both thought, *Why hadn't we been informed of this before?*

"Is there a time frame?" asked Nich, as if he had already known about the ongoing project.

"Funding has been a problem. Perhaps Lamda will add urgency to his request for more money."

Akio withheld asking why Murakami had never told him about his genome project. Because of Dr. Okawa's close relationship with Murakami, Akio didn't want to chance offending either of them.

"Could you advise us what you believe we should do about Lamda?" asked Nich.

"We're in a wait and see situation, wait for the genome to be mapped and see what's happening to Canada's salmon population. I'll be in touch with any new information as soon as it becomes available," promised Dr. Okawa.

Afterward, Okawa led them on a tour of his ultra-modern laboratory. When they passed by a closed, windowless door, they read its name plaque:

Dr. Masahiko Okawa
Private Laboratory

"Did you fertilized the eggs in this lab?" asked Nich, pointing to the door.

"This lab is my haven. Much like a den in your home, it contains everything I need to work, without the interruptions."

Dr. Okawa didn't answer Nich's question or extend an invitation for them to see inside. Both Akio and Nich still suspected the mutation occurred during the process of fertilization or shipment. Perhaps the solutions used to wash ova before fertilization caused the mutation. Nich asked a few more questions about processing. His questions were worded diplomatically to avoid even a hint of accusation.

Dr. Okawa provided more information, "I tried to simulate nature as close as possible. Hundreds of thousands of eggs arrived from the hatchery inside sterile containers bathed in their native river water. I washed the ova in the same Hokkaido river water where the spawning salmon would have laid their eggs, a precaution calculated to increase our chances of success. I've reasoned using sterilized saline solutions might add unnecessary risk to the procedure."

Both young researchers nodded. Dr. Okawa's method seemed reasonable.

The meeting ended. Dr. Okawa had addressed every topic on their minds. He never spoke to Akio directly, nor had Akio spoken to him. As they bid farewell, Okawa turned to Akio and said, "Dr. Naiporo, your work, your graduate school dissertation on ATP—quite impressive."

His comment surprised Akio. Both Okawa and Murakami must have read his dissertation on the relationship between the universal energy-producing substance, ATP, and aging. Akio thought, *Why would they be interested in the work of a graduate student?*

Nich and Akio drove back to the Agency in silence. They had come to a roadblock.

"Nich, do you think waiting for the coho genome is our only option? Should we be meeting with Dr. Murakami in Tokyo?"

"And take a chance on insulting Dr. Okawa? No, not a good idea, besides, Dr. Okawa said he would pass on to us any new information coming from the Imperial Institute."

Nich instructed Akio to return to Canada and continue to destroy all further *Lamdas*. He added, "Since the project is ending, the Canadians will soon take over responsibility for monitoring *Lamda's* effect on the salmon population."

Akio said, "I'm concerned *Lamda* could become an alpha variation of the species and upset the Pacific salmon's entire natural balance. Hundreds of *Lamdas* have already disseminated into Darwin's world where only the fittest survive."

21. The Throne

AKIO HAD RETURNED TO HIS PARENTS' CONDO AFTER SPENDING the day with Nich. His sister Yuri and her sixteen-year-old daughter, Hinata, had arrived from Sapporo. A prime-time program concerning an important issue gripping the country was about to air on national television—a woman's right to ascend to the *Chrysanthemum Throne*. After dinner, the family took chairs in front of the TV.

An amendment giving women the right to ascend to the Throne sat in the Japanese National Diet. It was undergoing the lengthy process leading to a vote by Japan's democratically chosen representatives. Tonight's national TV program intended to educate citizens on the pros and cons of the amendment.

The family listened to the moderator describe how the Imperial Family is governed by a different set of laws than the general laws applying to the rest of Japanese citizens. The current Imperial Household Law was passed by the Diet in 1947, under the American conquerors' watchful eyes. While it stripped away the Emperor's vast powers down to a ceremonial level, it retained the same rules of ascension formulated in 1889. The Emperor would be a male who serves until his death.

The moderator went on to explain, "Because our Diet is composed of too many political parties to include in this forum, we've invited two participants who represent the span of opposing views. Mr. Katsuro Yamaguchi is now serving his third term in the House of Representatives. He will educate us on the position endorsed by those in favor of allowing a female to become Empress and Mr. Yosio Sugawara will offer arguments against the proposed change."

A well-known popular activist for equal rights and progressive policies, Mr. Yamaguchi excelled at giving emotionally charged speeches. This handsome 48-year-old's youthful energy appealed to modern voters. He opened his remarks by pounding on the table and shouting,

"Eighty-six percent of Japanese people favor a woman's right to become the ruling Empress. Women already have equal rights under our present general law. Why don't they enjoy equal rights under Imperial Household law? Why don't women have an equal right to the Throne? The 1947 Imperial Household Law reflects anachronistic thinking based on 1889 attitudes. Women now hold influential positions in Japan, including in the Diet. Times have changed. The law should change to reflect our current values."

Although Mr. Yamaguchi went on for another twenty minutes, he made no other memorable points until raising two additional women's rights issues hidden in the proposed amendment: surrogacy and in vitro fertilization.

"Surrogacy is already being practiced in Japan although hasn't been written into law. A woman who can't bear children should have the legal right to loan her fertilized ova to a surrogate." He concluded by saying, "In vitro fertilization is another common practice. No formal law exists approving its use. I also believe a woman's right to IVF should be protected by law."

The live audience listened and applauded after the perspiring speaker finished. Akio and his family sat quietly in front of the TV.

Next, Mr. Sugawara gave his speech. A respected 75-year-old with three decades of service in the National Diet, he was an icon for traditional Japanese values. His conservative gray business suit matched his gray hair and mustache. He exhibited

130

a calm, dignified style, the same one which helped him build his reputation as a skilled negotiator. On the table in front of him sat a microphone ready to broadcast his voice to the entire country. Often looking at a teleprompter, he delivered his talk in a slow, deliberate tone.

"Mr. Moderator, my esteemed colleagues from the House of Representatives, and the Japanese people, it is my honor to present the dissenting opinion. In 660 B.C., Jimmu became the first Emperor of Japan. Legend tells us Jimmu descended directly from the sun goddess, Amaterasu. An unbroken line of 125 Emperors has followed. Since the Imperial Household Law of 1889, all have been male.

"Until the end of World War II, the Emperor had vast political power. Not only did people believe he descended from a god, many people thought him to be divine. During World War II, greedy men, who wanted to satisfy their self-serving goals, manipulated and abused the Emperor's trust. In the process, they almost destroyed our beloved country. As part of the surrender terms, the Emperor was forced to publicly announce he was not a god. Following the war, the Imperial Household Law of 1947 stripped the Emperor's power down to the ceremonial role it is today. One part of the 1889 Imperial Household Law remains: only a male can ascend to the Throne.

"Some of our people still believe the Emperor is a deity. Most regard the story as myth, passed on because it's a part of our historical tradition. Tradition forms the basis for a country's culture. We are steeped in our traditions. Consider our sport of sumo wrestling. Contestants still wear loincloths. Before each match, salt is thrown into the air to ward off evil spirits. Consider how we bow to each other, how we arise at sunrise on New Year's Day to welcome in the new year. Consider kimonos, traditional Japanese fashions, tea ceremonies, and tatami mats.

131

"A country should modernize and change with the times. Japan has changed. We are amongst the leaders of the modern world. Does changing with the times have to mean we must abandon the traditions of the past? Must we discard our beloved Bunraku puppets and replace them with Pikachu? Must we put typhoon-proof glass windows in the historic Horyuji Temple to satisfy a current building code? Yes, these traditions are old. Some label them anachronistic. Some say they serve no function in modern life, we can do without them.

"I beg to differ. Our traditions define who we are as Japanese. The Emperors' history is one of these traditions. Must we now abandon something defining us for over 2500 years to reconfirm women have equal rights? Must women act in the historical all-male performances at the Kabuki Theater to prove their equality? Must males perform in the all-female Takarazuka Revue to make the statement, 'men are equal, too?' Must men legislate themselves into the all-women Ama Pearl-divers to confirm their equality? I support equality for women. Succession to the Throne isn't about women's rights, it's about keeping our traditions alive."

After the program ended, a discussion started within the Naiporo family. When Yuri saw her father remained silent, she began, "I agree with Mr. Yamaguci. We're no longer in 1889. Succession to the Throne should reflect our changing times."

After making sure she wasn't interrupting, Mother said, "We don't need a new law. Amaterasu is the great female deity. She told us the Emperor will always be a male. I have faith in her."

Akio's father spoke next. His innate intelligence and a self-taught fund of knowledge belied his lack of formal education beyond high school. Although a dress shirt and tie had replaced his work clothes, he still traveled to work at the hatchery by bus. Instead of standing in cold water at sunrise, he now sat at a desk in an office with two other supervisors. The men working under him knew he had once toiled in each of their positions. His political opinion reflected the emotional scars inflicted on him during decades of bitter prejudice against the Indigenous Ainu people.

"It's difficult for me to put much faith in any of our representatives," he said.

"Why, Sofu?" asked Hinata.

"Why? We Ainu had no rights. We had to claw our way to where we are today. It took decades until our government recognized us an Indigenous people. Where were they before? How can I trust any of them? I'm feeling some hope now. The Ainu Party has joined the House of Representatives. Their voice will guide my vote."

"Thanks to you, we have it much easier," said Hinata. "What's your opinion, Uncle Akio?"

"Well, I support the women's rights movement but Mr. Sugawara's argument for keeping Japan's traditions alive struck home. Both arguments seem convincing. I'm torn." Akio added one more thought, "There's an elephant hiding in the room giving urgency to this amendment's outcome. The Crown Prince and Princess are in their fifties. They have one daughter and no sons. If the new law passes, their daughter could follow her father to the Crown."

After Yuri and Hinata left for home and Mother went to bed, Akio and his father stayed up to talk.

"Otosan, do you remember my dissertation partner in Canada?"

"Yes, a smart, polite, woman."

"She's still working in Vancouver. We've become close," Akio said, pausing for a response.

Father's expression changed to a look of concern. "I believe she is a native Canadian?"

"Yes, Otosan, she belongs to a tribe of Indigenous Peoples in Canada. Their history is similar to ours. The Indigenous People of Canada have endured terrible discrimination, just as the Ainu have here in Japan."

A period of silence followed. Father knew Akio wanted his approval.

"Akio, my son, the Canadians and Americans are more accepting of foreigners than the Japanese. Japanese who marry foreigners here are often treated as second-class citizens. If you add being Ainu, your difficulty will increase. You are my son. I don't want to see you hurt."

His answer wasn't what Akio wanted to hear. They nodded and went off to bed.

22. Canada

After returning to Canada, Akio met with Ken. While Akio described GenLife and the theory implicating a mutation on *Lamda's* X chromosome, Ken appeared nervous.

Fidgeting in his chair, he said, "Ottawa is more concerned with *Lamda's* effect on its salmon industry than details about a mutation. We want to know how to prevent *Lamda* from becoming a super fish capable of breeding out of control and destroying the entire native stock."

Akio knew Ken's rushed speech and inpatient tone reflected the pressure he felt from his superiors.

"I'm under the same pressure you are," Akio said. "*Lamda* is my responsibility. We tried to find answers during an interview with one of Japan's best minds in the field. He felt finding a solution to *Lamda* must wait for a map of the normal coho genome. He assured us our director in Tokyo is working on the project. Until completed, a wait and see approach is our only option."

"Canada has no interest in supporting or funding further research into the mutation," Ken snapped.

Sensing Ken's growing frustration, Akio changed his approach, "Have you seen any changes upstream? Are there any variations in the normal salmon population?"

"None, yet."

"Maybe there will be none. Except swimming upstream with all the spawners, *Lamda* has never showed any physical signs of spawning. *Lamdas* may never spawn, just die out naturally. Mutated genes would die with them."

"I hope you're right, Akio, my friend."

Ken's deep sigh indicated his reluctant acceptance of a wait-and-see approach.

Over the next few weeks, Akio closed the Japanese research division in Canada. In addition to sacrificing all returning *Lamdas*, Ken sent teams into the field to monitor the salmon population.

During the three weeks Akio spent closing out his project, Gwen realized phone calls from him were no substitute for being together. Marriage with Akio remained hypothetical. She never received an answer to why he cut the cord between them during those years after graduation. Only meeting by chance in the hatchery had reunited them. She felt she shared the responsibility for not reaching out to him either.

Gwen knew her father would say, "Don't dwell on it. Go on with your life; what's meant to be will happen." Gwen decided to wait, but not for much longer.

Akio returned to Vancouver. Although he arrived in the winter, homeless, jobless, and worried about *Lamda*, he felt these were some of his best days. Gwen took him in. Sharing new experiences made him feel even closer to her. He landed a job teaching Japanese at CU. Word spread among the undergraduates, especially among women. His classes filled within days of being posted. Only the conversation he had with his father about Gwen stood between him and his total happiness. Like two samurai dueling to the death, his positive thoughts about marriage fought with feelings of guilt from a marriage disapproved by his parents.

Nich's theory of a sex-linked mutation on the egg's X chromosome had confirmed Harriet's and Dr. Okawa's findings of an irregularity on the X chromosome. It couldn't have come at a better time. Increasing thoughts about death hounded Gwen. When death first became a reality, she had plenty of time to kick the can forward. At age thirty-one, the concept of death now changed from abstract to real. Uncovering *Lamda's* secret gave

136

her new hope of finding the secret to aging, hope for an antidote to her own death, and hope for freedom from the dread of thanatophobia. Only Murakami's map of the coho genome stood between her and restarting research on *Lamda*. The specimens Gwen had stored in her lab were waiting.

23. The Party of Amaterasu

CITING "FINANCIAL ISSUES," MURAKAMI REPORTED THE RESULTS of his genome project would be delayed at least another year. As a result, Gwen's research on *Lamda's* X chromosome had to be put on hold. At the same time political jockeying in Japan's National Diet delayed voting on the ascension bill, a related secret meeting took place in the exclusive Tokyo Kubo Plaza Hotel.

In a soundproofed room designed for the most sensitive occasions, five men sat in silence at the end of a rectangular mahogany table capable of seating twenty. Their dark business suits, stiff posture, clenched hands, and emotionless stares reflected the occasion's seriousness. Each man's glass of water, pad of paper, and pen were the room's sole amenities. To eliminate the risk of being recorded, cell phones were prohibited.

Nobody relaxed until Mr. Takashi Uchimura, Chairman of the Party of Amaterasu, started to talk from the head of the table.

"Gentleman, I called this emergency meeting to form a consensus concerning an issue of mutual concern. The opposition coalition's amendment to the Imperial Household Law of 1947 sits in the Diet awaiting a vote. Never has the male lineage to the Crown been as threatened as now. Our next Emperor, the Crown Prince, has no son. If the amendment passes, after the Crown Prince becomes Emperor and dies, his daughter could become the Empress. Our party strongly opposes any change to the historical male ascendancy law.

"We're in a secure location at the request of our special guest, a man who is one of the most powerful leaders in the

138

House of Representatives. He shares our views on ascension and is in a stronger position than any of us to sway members of the controlling coalition. He requested his presence at this meeting be kept secret for fear leaks about conferring with our party might jeopardize his political standing as a moderate. For the record, I suggest we refer to him by the code name, *Sushi*."

Looking around the room for hidden microphones, *Sushi* appeared nervous. In a rushed voice, he said, "Gentlemen, let me get to the point. We must act together in opposing a change to the present law. I'm against the amendment allowing women to ascend to the Throne and oppose legalizing both surrogacy and in vitro fertilization. Do I have your support?"

Mr. Uchimura answered first, "I share your view against changing the ascendancy law. I prefer to leave surrogacy and in vitro as they are now, practiced, but not addressed by law."

Sushi nodded his agreement. The rest remained expressionless. "And your opinion, Dr. Murakami?"

Dr. Nabuo Murakami, the same man who directed the Japanese section of the Joint Fisheries Project, was a staunch supporter of the Party of Amaterasu. His considerable family money added to his influence on their policies.

In contrast with the neutral business-mask he wore on his face throughout his professional life, this short skeletal man stood up to vent his anger. "I oppose the amendment," he barked as if picking a fight. "From the time Emperor Shōwa assumed the Crown, through his reign during World War II, zealots in the military and in the government exploited him. At the war's end, the Emperor took responsibility for their disaster. Hasn't the position of Emperor been diminished enough? We should not further dilute Japan's most sacred tradition. Regarding the issues of surrogacy and in vitro fertilization, being chairman of the in vitro department at the Imperial Institute of Genetics, I abstain from voicing a position."

The next to speak was Mr. Kubo. He had made billions in real estate holdings. The Tokyo Kubo Plaza stood as the flagship for his international hotel conglomerate. An avid supporter of the far-right's ideology, he helped fund the inception of the Party of Amaterasu. With his usual air of polished confidence, he said, "My colleagues, welcome to the Tokyo Kubo Plaza. I pledge my continued support for our chairman's ideology. I thank you, *Sushi*, for your support and hope I can be of assistance to your reelection efforts."

The last speaker, Dr. Masahiko Okawa, had been an ideological supporter of the Party of Amaterasu since its inception. He and his former scientific protege, Dr. Murakami, shared old-school, devout, Shinto beliefs. He felt a male-only succession to the Crown was the will of Amaterasu. As a renowned scientist, when in public Dr. Okawa kept his political opinions private. At these political meetings, his opinions enjoyed the ear of Mr. Uchimura.

In the same low-key convincing tone as when he met with Akio and Nich, he said, "We have an uphill battle. Public sentiment is shifting towards the pro-amendment side. Many voters view male lineage as a violation of women's rights. Having Sushi and his controlling coalition on our side, helps. Nevertheless, to win, we'll need to attract moderates. Depending on the polls, I would keep open to the possibility of conceding smaller issues in exchange for the bigger prize. If necessary, we could support legalizing in vitro and surrogacy in exchange for keeping the ascension law as it stands."

Mr. Uchimura said, "*Sushi*, we're unanimous, we're with you."

The meeting ended. *Sushi* checked his watch and left first. Having secured the support of this fringe party, he couldn't wait to leave. Rushing to the door, he hoped nobody would discover he'd been there. The others talked among themselves until released by Mr. Uchimura ten minutes later.

24. Surprise at the Peacock

SITTING AT THE PEACOCK BAR ONE LATE FRIDAY AFTERNOON, Gwen looked troubled. She said to Akio, "A question you've never answered still bothers me. After graduation, I heard almost nothing from you for five years."

Including those five years, they had known each other for eleven; four in graduate school as lab partners and friends, the last two bonding romantically in Vancouver.

"When your airline connections went through Vancouver on your trips to the hatchery, why didn't you call me? As a close friend, I felt excluded from your life."

The question stopped Akio in his tracks. Earlier in the afternoon, he plotted a scheme with the bartender to surprise Gwen. A detour sign forced his speeding car to turn in another direction.

"I should have apologized before. The reason wasn't for lack of affection. My parents opposed our friendship reaching another level. They used the words 'disappointment' and 'embarrassment' to describe a Japanese-foreigner union. My feelings for you conflicted with their expectations. When I didn't hear from you, I assumed your feelings for me weren't any deeper than many friendships made during school, ones fading away as friends move on with their lives. In my culture, respect for parents has a strong influence on Japanese children. I feared if I followed my heart and reignited our relationship, both of us could be hurt."

Gwen now understood. Leaning over on her bar stool, she kissed him. Their friendship and romance had matured into love.

Relieved, Akio's wink to the bartender signaled time for action. Without asking for an order, he served up two tall glasses of Guinness, each inscribed with a foam heart. Akio lifted his glass and said, "Gwen, I love you. Will you marry me?"

A prolonged hug across the barstools answered his question. The bartender's announcement elicited a round of cheers from the local barflies and waitstaff. Later in the evening, Gwen had a fleeting thought. *When two mutts breed, one Japanese-Ainu and the other First Nations-Irish Catholic, Darwin would jump with joy over our children's genetic strength.*

Planning the wedding had its problems. Gwen's parents accepted their daughter's decision to intermarry. Akio's weren't supportive. On his visit home to announce their engagement, he sought his parents' approval. He knew their reluctance wasn't personal. They had met Gwen only for a brief time during her dissertation in Vancouver.

"We didn't get to know her, but I remember she's a beautiful woman," said Akio's mother. "Her long, shiny, black hair and smooth skin made me think she might have some Japanese blood."

His father again warned about the hardships Akio would face in Japan by marrying a foreigner.

Akio said, "Otosan, I appreciate the sacrifices you've made for me. Times are changing. People in Japan are more accepting of foreigners now than they were in years past. Neither Yuri nor I faced more than a whisper of prejudice. Yuri's children feel equal to their peers."

His parents' opposition to an intermarriage puzzled Akio. He knew his father and grandfather had intermarried. Akio wondered if his father felt another intermarriage would take the family's assimilation too far or perhaps dilute their ten thousand year Ainu ancestry closer to the point of extinction. Akio's mother's disapproval stemmed from other factors. She adhered to Shinto's pre-war, xenophobic view of foreigners. Only obedience to her husband's wishes could change her opinion.

"Gwen and I both share a deep respect for our parents. We're proud of our Indigenous ancestries. We intend to keep our traditions alive and pass them down to our children," said Akio. His validation of his father's worry hit home. Hearing Ainu culture would be passed on, a look of relief spread over his father's face.

Another obstacle for Akio's parents was shame. They feared some guests invited to a Japanese wedding might disapprove of the marriage.

"Otōsan, I plan to be married in Canada before flying here for a family celebration."

Removing some of the worry from their parents' shoulders ended the impasse. Although his parents reluctantly approved, Akio's guilt over assimilation continued.

25. The Vote

SOON AFTER GWEN'S AND AKIO'S ENGAGEMENT, THE DIET VOTED on the female succession amendment. Walking along a street in Vancouver with Gwen, Akio bought a Japanese newspaper and checked the results. He translated the article word-for-word to Gwen.

"The new law:

> 1) continues unchanged the male-only succession to the Throne
> 2) mandates reconsideration of male-only succession every ten years
> 3) legalizes surrogacy
> 4) legalizes in vitro fertilization

Neither the conservative wing nor the liberal opposition had enough votes to win without a compromise. As in a fair divorce agreement, those pro and con feel equally cheated. The pros are complaining the present succession rules should have been changed. The cons oppose legalizing surrogacy and in vitro fertilization. The democratic system imposed on Japan after WW-II is the real winner. A compromise has been reached, without violence and without a coup."

"What do you think, Gwen?"
"Disappointed."

26. Matsutake

As Gwen and Akio continued to make wedding plans, the time had come for Akio to meet Gwen's parents at their home in Three Peaks. What started with awkward formality at dinner, ended in a bonding friendship.

After coffee the next morning, Gwen's parents joined them for a hike to Sparkle Lake. They planned to retrace the path Gwen had so often rode with her father on Gypsy. Carrying backpacks, they first took Akio on a short walk from the house to the Skeena River. He gazed up across the water at a panorama of lush mountains filled with subalpine firs and tall lodgepole pines. When he took his first look above the tree line and saw the glacier-capped Three Peaks Mountain, he felt the magnetic hold this area had on generations of Indigenous Peoples.

On the way to Sparkle Lake, they detoured off the trail down a narrow deer track leading to Frank's secret mushroom spot. "See that little mound," said Frank pointing to a raised clump of moss at the base of a Douglas fir. Mary dug her hands under the mound to uncover a beautiful pine mushroom. It's white cap sat on top of a long stem. Mother sniffed it and handed it to Akio. "Take a whiff. This species has a giveaway smell."

Akio took a sniff, "Cinnamon?"

"You're right, the pickers call it 'red hot and dirty socks,' the smell of cinnamon candy mixed with dirt."

Akio remembered the smell. When he was a boy, he had often tagged along with his grandfather to work at the Hokkaido Mushroom plant. His grandfather toiled most of his adult life at almost every step of the business, from a field laborer to sales.

Frank said, "This mushroom is a pine mushroom. It's almost the same as the matsutake in Japan. In Canada, we call it by either name."

Akio knew far more about these mushrooms than he let on. He had learned about them from his grandfather. Later in life, when Akio was a senior studying botany at Hokkaido University, he tried and failed to grow matsutakes indoors. He intended to continue in that direction during grad school until a tuition-free scholarship to CU's biotech program became irresistible.

Not wanting to upstage the Naiporos, he limited his response, "They're a delicacy in Japan. People associate them with long life and digestive health."

While foraging, Gwen dug up a few more similar to the ones her mother had dug. "See how these fungi live near the tree's roots," she said to Akio.

"What's this one?" Akio asked Gwen after uncovering one looking different.

"It's a baby pine mushroom in its early button stage. It's covered by a membrane resembling a veil."

"It looks as if it's been shrink-wrapped. Should I put it back?" Akio asked, as if he didn't know.

"Only if you want to throw away money. The button stage is the tastiest and most valuable. We export the highest grades of matsutakes to Japan; the higher the grade, the higher the price."

Akio knew the quantity of matsutakes harvested in Japan had plummeted over the past twenty years. The Canadian exporters knew the Japanese taste for them didn't. The price soared as Japan imported many of British Columbia's best quality mushrooms.

Frank joined the conversation. "October to late November is the best time for picking in this area. Pickers start in the north and work their way south."

He went on to describe the often hostile competition between native and itinerant pickers. Gwen had never seen her father talk and smile as much, a clear testimony to his comfort level with Akio. It seemed sharing aboriginal origins added to their budding kinship.

When Gwen's parents walked ahead, Gwen told Akio about her father's mushroom business.

"He's been picking pine mushrooms on First Nation's land a long time. What started as his hobby became a seasonal business. In six weeks, he earns more from this side job than he earns in four months as a large vehicle mechanic."

I'd be interested in hearing more about your father's business."

Gwen answered, "His secret to success is cutting out the middlemen. Mushrooms go through several steps between picking and your plate."

"Your father is a picker?"

"A picker and more: a sorter, cleaner, transporter, and seller. He knows Vancouver's large Asian population pays top dollar for matsutakes. Avoiding middlemen, he sells his mushrooms direct to the local restaurants and markets. They receive a high-quality product at a lower cost. Their customers receive the quality they want and Father makes more money."

Akio expressed a strong interest in learning more. He and Frank made plans to meet during his next sales trip to Vancouver.

Two weeks later, Frank packed over two hundred pounds of pine mushrooms in the bed of his pickup truck. When he arrived in Vancouver, he stopped at Gwen's apartment to meet Akio. Now on a first-name basis, Akio and Frank planned their sales stops. They would visit businesses paying the most first before continuing down their list and selling out.

The first stop at Hinaka Japanese Cuisine brought them into the Asian section of downtown.

"Ah, Mr. Sunrise, what a pleasure to see you again," said Mr. Kobayashi, with a shallow bow. The distinguished-looking owner wore a formal black suit and necktie. His attire at lunchtime reflected the restaurant's prices. Frank and Akio wore work boots and jeans.

Father responded with a shallow bow and said, "I want to introduce you to a new friend of our family, Dr. Akio Naiporo from Hokkaido, Japan." Mr. Kobayashi's eyes opened wide with surprise, precipitating a flourish of conversation with Akio in Japanese. After a few minutes, the owner caught himself and apologized, "I'm sorry Mr. Sunrise. It's a treat for me to meet someone with whom I have so much in common. We've been talking about our mutual interest in mushrooms and Japan." Father gave an approving smile. Looking at Akio, the owner said, "Mr. Sunrise never disappoints. His are the highest grade matsutakes in Canada."

Mr. Kobayashi introduced the chef. After the owner left, the chef walked with Frank and Akio out the kitchen door to the truck. Picking a few mushrooms from the load, the chef examined each one in the light, smelled it, and felt its texture. After breaking off a piece, he savored the taste. "My customers love your mushrooms," said the chef. Frank and Akio unloaded thirty-five pounds at sixty-five dollars per pound. Cooked to perfection, the restaurant could easily earn a four hundred percent profit.

After visiting five more Japanese restaurants, four Asian food markets, and two street vendors, they drove south about forty minutes to Richmond. They sold their last thirty pounds to British Columbia Mushroom, a large export company.

Before falling asleep, Gwen whispered into Akio's ear, "I think you may have found your passion." She was right. Akio's interest in the mushroom business increased as he drifted further away from his Ph.D. degree.

27. The Reception

ARMED WITH PHOTOS FROM THEIR RECENT WEDDING AT THREE Peaks, Gwen and Akio were flying to a reception at his parents' condo in Hokkaido. "I'm nervous. I may do or say something offensive. Any advice?" asked Gwen.

"Neither of my parents speaks a word of English. Yuri and I will be there to translate. I believe the term in English is, 'We've got your back.' Be yourself, and you'll have no problems."

Gwen asked the same questions again while staying at Yuri's house in Sapporo. Yuri added one piece of advice, "Help clear the table with the rest of us, no matter how much my father protests."

They drove to the Naiporo's the next day. Their second-floor condo looked out onto a dreary working-class complex of four-story buildings. It looked as if every building had been constructed from the same gray Legos blocks. Each weather-beaten old structure contained sixteen identical units with a small balcony looking out at another condo building.

Carrying gifts up the stairs, Yuri's family followed Akio and Gwen to a double locked front door. Akio unlocked the door which led into a small entry area. Gwen and Akio exchanged their shoes for slippers before passing through a decorative curtain separating the entryway from the condo's main room. The rest followed in turn. Wearing a dark business suit and carrying a vase of cherry blossoms, Akio walked to greet his parents. Gwen followed in a floral, mid-length dress. Yuri and her husband with two young children entered last.

Akio's father, Shigeru Naiporo, had on the same suit he

151

wore at the dissertations. Akio's mother, Shizue, wore a traditional kimono. Both Gwen and Akio had expected to see other relatives and family friends. None were there.

"Otosan and Okasan, this is my wife, Gwen Sunrise Naiporo. We've looked forward to sharing our happiness with you," said Akio. He spoke first in Japanese, then in English. To convey respect, Gwen bowed without making eye contact. Bending from her waist, with her hands overlapped in front, she first honored Mr. Naiporo, then Akio's mother. The parents returned shallow bows. Mrs. Naiporo gave a polite smile and extended her hand to Gwen. His father did the same without the smile. Akio was proud of his wife. He knew her straight posture, air of sophistication, and quiet confidence wasn't an act.

"I have fond memories of meeting you at Canada University," Gwen said while Akio translated. "My mother and father send you their best wishes. My father often talks about how much he enjoyed his conversation with you about salmon and mushrooms."

Mr. Naiporo's face softened as he acknowledged the compliment with a shallow bow. Akio handed Gwen the bouquet of Japanese cherry blossoms they bought on the ride from Sapporo. Because gifts are traditionally exchanged later in the evening, Akio explained these flowers had special significance. His real worry was them wilting if not put in water.

Having been coached by Akio and Yuri on Japanese customs, Gwen gifted the flowers with two hands. "Cherry blossoms first came to North America as a gift of friendship from Japan to Washington, D.C. They symbolize my hopes for a lasting friendship with you."

Mrs. Naiporo accepted them with two hands, "Oh, you shouldn't have gone through the trouble."

After greeting Yuri and her family, Mrs. Naiporo led

152

everyone to the Kamidana. Although this wasn't a wedding, she wanted to observe a few traditional Shinto wedding customs. A tray containing three stacked ceremonial saki cups sat on a low table. She clapped twice, bowed, and prayed to the Kami,

"We seek the blessing and protection of the Kami for our son Akio and his bride, Gwendolyn."

She poured saki into one cup and passed it to Akio. He took three sips, bowed, and handed it to Gwen. He whispered in her ear to copy him. She took three sips. Mrs. Naiporo filled up the second cup; they repeated the same ritual twice. Akio passed each cup to each of his parents. Each took a sip. One more clap and they sat down to eat and drink more saki.

Akio's mother had prepared one of his favorite meals: Japanese curry and Niku-jyaga, a traditional meat and potatoes dish. After dinner, when Gwen saw Yuri and her mother working in the kitchen, she stood up to help. Father gave a soft command in Japanese.

Akio translated, "He told you not to help because you're the guest of honor."

Gwen bowed and said, "You are kind." She walked to the kitchen. This interaction helped Mr. Naiporo realize the difference between modern women and those of his generation. He saw the similarities between Yuri and Gwen; both were modern women; respectful, strong, and independent.

At Akio's request, his mother unwrapped Gwen's present of a hand-carved totem depicting a deer, a bear, and a salmon. "This totem was carved by a craftsman from my people. The deer, bear, and salmon played important parts in both First Nations and Ainu history," said Gwen. Mr. Naiporo handed Akio a special envelope containing money.

Gwen and Akio soon left for Sapporo with Yuri's family. The two tired children were ready to leave. The following day,

Akio and Gwen rented a car to visit Hokkaido Mushroom with Mr. Naiporo. When Mr. Naiporo introduced Gwen as his daughter-in-law, he paid close attention to the peoples' reactions. To his relief, he saw nobody appearing judgmental about his son marrying a foreigner.

Although Akio's grandfather was no longer alive, the owner remembered him fondly. During the conversation, Akio described Three Peaks Mushroom and his father-in-law's success in starting a business capable of shipping matsutakes directly to Japan. "I'm involved with a mushroom business in Canada. We hope to export quality matsutake mushrooms at lower prices than your current suppliers." The owner's enthusiasm led to lunch, a walk around a nearby park, and a series of bows and handshakes. They planned to stay in contact as Three Peaks Mushroom grew.

Their honeymoon on the main island of Honshu included a tour of the Imperial Palace. Unknown to them, inside the palace, an event was taking place which would affect Gwen's life and perhaps all life on earth.

28. In Vitro

WHILE THE NEWLYWEDS TOURED THE IMPERIAL PALACE, NEARBY in the Imperial Institute of Genetics, Dr. Murakami personally carried a labeled container from the ultra-secure specimen storage room. Dwarfed between two muscular armed guards and accompanied by a woman scribe, this diminutive man walked straight to the Imperial Hospital's obstetric unit. After changing into scrubs, he entered the operating room and handed the container to Dr. Tonegawa, chief obstetrician-gynecologist for the Imperial Family. On the operating table lay a twenty-five-year-old Royal princess. She wore a mask concealing her identity and at the same time allowing Dr. Tonegawa and the anesthetist to observe her airway. Only Dr. Murakami, the donors, and her parents knew her identity.

The container held fertilized ova from a donor couple. Before performing the in vitro implantation, the doctor and the operating room nurse confirmed her wrist band numbers matched the numbers on the record. A coded label on the specimen container kept the donors' identities secret. Only Dr. Murakami, the donors, the patient, and her parents knew their names.

A guard waited outside the procedure room while a scribe stood in the background recording the entire process. Dr. Tonegawa completed the in vitro implant successfully. The fast-acting sedative wore off in minutes, soon leaving the patient awake and alert. After an hour of observation, with her mask still in place, the patient was wheeled out of the hospital into a private car. Obscured by tinted windows, the car sped away with her father driving and her mother at the Princess's side in the backseat.

The usual whispered buzzing amongst the staff could only offer guesses about the recipient's and donors' identities. Dr. Murakami returned to his lab and life in Japan went on as usual.

Nine months later, an announcement from Japan shocked the entire world.

29. Prince Hitomu

NINE MONTHS AFTER THAT SECRET IN VITRO FERTILIZATION, AKIO was in Vancouver surfing the net during a break between teaching Japanese classes. Always interested in affairs happening in his native country, he was aware significant changes in the Imperial House had occurred during the past year. The ailing Emperor had died and his son, the Crown Prince, had become Emperor. He and the Empress still had a daughter and no son. While sitting in front of his laptop, Akio received a newsflash released by the Imperial House:

> "The Emperor and Empress announced the birth of their son at 2 P.M yesterday. Crown Prince Hitomu weighed 7.4 pounds. He is in excellent health. The Prince is now next in line to follow his father to the Chrysanthemum Throne."

Akio looked at a picture of the smiling Empress, holding her baby. She stood alongside her husband and twenty-nine-year-old daughter.

Impossible, thought Akio, shaking his head in disbelief, *The Empress is beyond her childbearing years. She's been unable to bear children since the birth of her daughter.*

He continued reading,

> "The surrogate for the Empress was a Royal Princess from a family having direct lineage to the Crown. She felt blessed Amaterasu chose her

to help continue the male line of succession. Her family requests their identity remain unknown."

Over the next few days, Akio and Gwen often checked their computers for more breaking news. Information released by the Imperial House to the media validated the event's legality. In 2003, the Crown Prince and Princess requested their ova and sperm be harvested and stored. Dr. Okawa, then Director of In Vitro Fertilization at the Imperial Institute of Genetics, carried out their request. Nine months ago, as ordered by the royal couple, embryos from those gametes were implanted into the surrogate using in vitro methods. As was customary, no further comments from the Imperial House were forthcoming.

Akio and all of Japan read and listened to the announcement in disbelief. He remembered the new law upholding male-only eligibility to the Crown would be reviewed in ten years. If the law isn't upheld at that time, without a son, the Emperor's daughter could have succeeded him to the Throne. Akio now understood: Prince Hitomu's birth eliminated that possibility and assured the next emperor would be male.

This birth announcement brought mixed opinions. The naysayers claimed the eggs and sperm didn't belong to the Crown Prince and Princess. They argued a Crown Prince couldn't be born out of surrogacy and said in vitro techniques couldn't be used in Royal births.

The amendment legalizing in vitro fertilization and surrogacy negated most of those criticisms. Publication of the meticulous documentation that recorded each step in the process, plus DNA proof, squelched the rest. Attempts made by the press to uncover any dirt from the Imperial Hospital's staff came to no avail.

Doctors Okawa and Murakami received praise for their roles as pioneers in vitro fertilization. They declined interviews. A released statement read:

> "These two honorable servants to the Imperial House request their right to privacy be respected."

30. The Hunt

GWEN HAD BEEN AT AN IMPASSE WAITING FOR MURAKAMI'S MAP of the coho genome. The news of Crown Prince Hitomu's birth jolted Akio and Gwen as if their alarm clock screamed, *Wake up, wake up, you've been sleeping for three years. Now can you figure it out?* Gwen began thinking about Hitomu's in vitro birth. *Could it be related to* Lamda? *Did legalizing in vitro and surrogacy fit into the same puzzle?*

They hadn't waited long when several related events catapulted them back into the hunt for *Lamda's* secret. Akio's cell phone rang. He had just returned home from playing baseball with his Sunday adult-league. "Akio, it's Nich. I couldn't wait to share the news. I received Ken Rosenstat's four-year follow-up report concerning project cohos returning to the River of No Return. *Lamdas* stopped returning," he said, raising his voice a few octaves with excitement. "Those, making it upstream past the hatchery, progressively disappeared at a rate consistent with natural causes. The last one my team spotted was being eaten by a bear. Even better, they've seen no abnormal changes in the entire native male and female salmon populations."

Putting down his baseball glove and sweaty hat, Akio said, "You mean either the *Lamdas* never spawned or. . ."

"It means we are off the hook," interrupted a gleeful Nich. "I'm sure Dr. Murakami, Okawa, and the Fisheries Ministry are delighted as well."

Akio smiled at the hook pun before asking, "What do you think caused *Lamda*?"

"Akio, my friend, as much as I want to help you and Gwen solve the *Lamda* mystery, it's too risky for me. Being involved in an investigation of powerful individuals here in Japan could prove professionally disastrous. Since the project has ended, I need to bow out."

Akio knew the report meant both the Japanese and Canadian involvement in the project had ended. The *Lamda* issue disappeared. Japan and Canada considered the study successful. It demonstrated environmental factors, rather than their genetic makeup, had guided the returning cohos to their spawning beds. Although the *Lamda* issue disappeared for those involved in the Joint Fisheries Project, it didn't go away for Gwen. She still saw *Lamda* as a possible exciting link to discovering a pathway to immortality.

Soon after Nich's call, a second event occurred. At last, Dr. Murakami's laboratory released the results of his long-awaited coho genome map. The entire genome became available to the world. The wall blocking further investigation into the X chromosome mutation no longer stood in the way. Gwen wondered if the timing of Murakami's coho genome release was a coincidence or was connected to Hitomu's birth.

Within days after the genome release, Gwen received a phone call from the Francis D. O'Connor Laboratory for Genome Science, a private lab in Vancouver. Although they had received *Lamda* specimens from her earlier in her research, they couldn't continue without the comparison data to the normal genome. "Dr. Sunrise, we received the coho genome map and will go back to work on your *Lamda* tomorrow."

"I'm still concerned about a possible mutation on the X chromosome," Gwen reminded her colleague at the O'Connor lab.

"We're on it, Dr. Sunrise."

A smile crossed Gwen's face as she put her phone back into her purse.

Weeks later, she received their twenty-page report comparing *Lamda's* chromosomes with a normal male Pacific coho's. The conclusion stated:

> A mutation found on the X chromosome of an XY male coho salmon labeled '*Lamda*' is located on the promoter gene directly adjacent to the ATPase gene complex. Since there is no previous data documenting gene mutations in Pacific coho salmon, we can't determine if the mutation is a spontaneous event or a segment added by gene-editing techniques. If a similar sequence appeared in humans, its structure would be more consistent with having been genetically engineered. The genome is otherwise typical for a two to three-year-old, ocean-phase coho.

Although feeling elated, Gwen thought she shouldn't share this sensitive information with anyone except Akio. Carrying home a bag filled with dirty lab coats for the washing machine, she rushed to tell him the news. When she opened the door, what she saw replaced her thoughts about *Lamda* with the reality of everyday married life. Wearing one of her aprons, Akio stood in front of the stove stirring Japanese food in a wok. His night to cook usually meant reheating Japanese take-out. A laugh and a kiss said everything about their marriage. Brimming with excitement, she couldn't hold off any longer. "Big news. The O'Connor report confirms our theory of an X chromosome abnormality. It's on the ATPase promoter gene."

Akio nodded his head to acknowledge he had heard her news. Facing the risk of a victory arm-pump upsetting the wok, he limited his response to, "Great news," while continuing to stir. After turning off the stove, he said, "Your suspicions were correct. It sounds like a manufactured gene inserted into the X chromosome. Now we need to figure out a relationship between the promoter gene and *Lamda*."

Gwen said, "I've worked with other promoter genes. This one regulates the ATPase gene, an enzyme essential for the production of energy in the form of ATP. The promoter is similar to a gas pedal controlling the amount of gas injected when more speed is needed. The promoter gene orders the ATPase gene to produce more ATP when more energy is needed."

After dinner, they sat down to figure out the link between this mutation and an ageless salmon. Instead of being classmates working on their Ph.D. dissertations, they were married scientists at home working on mortality, a problem plaguing Gwen for most of her life and puzzling humanity for its recorded history.

Still sitting around the kitchen table, Akio flashed back to his meeting with Dr. Okawa at GenLife. "After Dr. Okawa led us on a tour, he spoke to me for the first time. He told me he had read our dissertation on ATP. He must have had an interest in the relationship between genes and ATP."

In a voice trying to keep up with her thoughts, Gwen said, "And his protege, Dr. Murakami, had an interest in aging research and ATP. He wrote an ATP study into the coho project. I doubt his choice to stage the Japanese section near Okawa's lab in Hokkaido was a coincidence."

Gwen paused while thinking steps ahead. "I understand why there were no female *Lamdas* in the first generation. Only males in the first generation with the mutation would express the modified gene. Because both X chromosomes in a female need to be effected to be expressed, no females *Lamdas* would appear in the first generation. In subsequent generations, two mutated X chromosomes would have joined by chance causing both female and male *Lamdas* to appear.

While trying to solve Gwen's question, Akio resembled an American football coach in the locker room at half-time. Instead of Xs and Os designating the players on opposing teams, he wrote Xs and Ys on a piece of paper attached to his clipboard. "Ah hah," he gloated, "If *Lamdas* didn't spawn, they couldn't pass down the mutation. Nich believed *Lamdas* never spawned and Ken's team observed all the *Lamdas* died from natural causes."

"Even if *Lamdas* didn't spawn," Gwen said, "many of the female cohos still carried the mutation on one of their two X chromosomes. After a few generations of natural breeding with normal males, females with both X chromosomes would have been born. They would have expressed the trait. They didn't. All *Lamdas* died naturally as if the mutation was never passed on. There were no further ageless males or females seen in subsequent generations."

She paused to think about the validity of her statement. Akio did the same by writing more Xs and Ys on his clipboard.

"Humm, you're right," he said. Let's expand on your theory. What if the modified promoter genes were locked, silent, and not expressed when they left GenLife? Most species, including humans, contain an enormous number of silent genes never expressed. They act as if they're piano keys with no strings to play. What if Okawa's engineered genes were locked when inherited? They would stay silent when passed down through subsequent generations. Only if the gene became unlocked, would the mutation appear. Unless unlocked, all the altered genes in the first or in future generations would carry a silent gene and not expressed.

164

"What if, somehow, the cohos sent from Okawa's lab became unlocked? Only one generation of ageless males would be born. Even when unlocked, the females carrying only one mutated X chromosome wouldn't show the trait. In subsequent generations, male or female cohos inheriting the altered gene wouldn't exhibit any abnormal traits because those genes would have been locked. That's what we observed. Males showed the trait for only one generation, females never showed it."

Exhausted from their rapid-fire mental gymnastics, they slumped back in their chairs and took a couple of deep breaths. After a pause, Gwen rephrased their new theory to ensure she understood. "You're saying the X chromosome of the ova at GenLab was genetically modified before being fertilized by normal, unaltered sperm. Once fertilized, Okawa sent the embryos to you in Canada."

"Yes," said Akio.

"They grew in your hatchery before being released into the river. During their second year in the ocean, the engineered promoter gene somehow unlocked."

"Yes"

"The gene remained locked until being unlocked. At the time, these fish were swimming in the ocean in their prime of life, similar to an eighteen to twenty-one-year-old humans. How were the engineered genes unlocked in the middle of the ocean? Who turned the key on *Lamda*?"

"Good question," Akio said while shrugging his shoulders to give Gwen the "I don't know" sign. "Since the fish lived in the ocean at the time, maybe tiny scuba divers followed all the salmon around with a syringe, waiting to inject them at the right time."

To his disappointment, his attempt at humor received only an indifferent gesture from Gwen. While Akio thought of ways to improve his joke, Gwen fixated on his word—inject. "What about the Coded Wire Tracker? Wasn't one injected into every project fish?"

An explosion erupted in Akio's mind. He recalled the light blue CWT wire on the spools sent to him from Japan. "I had assumed the colored coating allowed better penetration into their snouts. I remember the blue color had dissolved completely by the time the salmon returned to the project. Only bare, stainless steel wire remained."

A phone call to Nich followed, "Nich, I have new information about *Lamda*. As you requested, I promised not to share it with you. I only want to know who made the CWTs and who ordered them."

Nich answered, "Dr. Murakami ordered them from a company called Wire Tokyo, Inc. Their shipment went straight to you in Canada."

"Thanks, Nich. I'll look into it."

Within days Akio had made an appointment with the company. He booked a plane for Tokyo.

31. Wire Tokyo

AKIO HELD ONTO HIS SEAT AS THE CAB SPED THROUGH AN industrial area of Tokyo. Arriving at his destination, he saw a two-story, rectangular warehouse with rows of tall windows lining both its long sides. Written in large Japanese symbols, a sign over the front entrance read: Wire Tokyo.

Akio walked inside. From the outside, he thought the building consisted of two separate floors. Instead, on the inside, he saw one massive open space occupying the entire building. The fifty by seventy-five-meter interior contained an entire room filled with symmetrical rows of wire-making machinery, work tables, and storage containers. Wire spools ranging in size from sewing machine bobbins to bridge cables were stacked in order of function and size. A kaleidoscope of copper, red, white, black, green, and blue insulation livened the otherwise drab workspace. Looking up at the ceiling, Akio saw pipes, ventilation ducts, and wires snaking through a maze of catwalks.

Akio knocked on a door inscribed with *Office*.

"Come in," invited Mr. Hideo Yagi from his desk inside the glass-enclosed room. He was the supervisor Akio had phoned from Vancouver. In his thirties, this well-groomed man, about Akio's age, stood up from behind his desk and introduced himself. They bowed before exchanging business cards. "Dr. Naiporo, I hope your flight from Canada went well. Welcome back to Japan."

"Thank you, sir, I'm happy to be back eating real Japanese food."

Mr. Yagi smiled and continued, "I looked up the sales records for the Canadian Joint Fisheries Study Project. If you could excuse me, I'm required to ask you for identification before releasing information. I'm sorry."

Akio handed him his passport and papers supporting his position as director of the Japanese clinical branch of the project in British Columbia.

"Thank you, Doctor Naiporo. According to our records, we shipped four spools of coded wire trackers to you in British Columbia. They were ordered four months before they were shipped. The order instructed us to send them to you before April. Did everything go well?"

"Yes, Mr. Yagi. We received them as ordered, in excellent condition. May I ask who ordered them?"

"Let me see," he responded, pausing to scroll down his computer screen. "Ah, here's the signature: Dr. N-a-b. . . Sorry, I can't read his penmanship. I met the gentleman and have forgotten his name."

He spun his computer around for Akio to read.

"Oh, yes, Dr. Nabuo Murakami. He's the director of the entire Japanese project."

"Yes, that was his name."

Akio's mind drifted momentarily to question how this wire was able to deliver a substance capable of unlocking the promoter gene.

Mr. Yagi broke the silence, "May I show you where we made the wire?"

They walked to an area marked *Medical Division*.

"This small machine, resembling a sump pump, churned out your stainless steel CWT wire through a tiny hole. Inside the machine, a laser inscribed its code. After the wire exited the machine, it wound itself around spools."

Akio waited before asking a lingering question, "A light blue substance covered the wire I received. Can you explain?"

Mr. Yagi paused, stroked his chin, and answered, "Ah, yes, now I remember. That gave us a real challenge. Dr. Murakami visited us to ask if we could apply a thin coat of solution to the wire. He said it was a vitamin. If I remember correctly, he said it was folic acid. After its application, he wanted an insulating material, similar to electrical wiring, to cover the CWT. My most difficult challenge was his requirement for the insulation to dissolve in three or four years. He explained to me the wire would be embedded internally in the salmon's snout. He wanted to see if the released folic acid would alter the salmon's growth while it swam in the ocean.

"The solution arrived in a sterile container labeled *Folic Acid Solution*. We adapted our machine to spray the solution onto the wire before coating it with a blue, quick-drying insulation material. We hoped it would disintegrate within his time frame. Since we manufacture many wires for use in microsurgical procedures, difficult challenges such as this are common for us. We used our experience with wire insulation and drug eluting medical stents. How did we do?"

"You did well, sir," answered Akio. "When we injected the CWT into each fish's snout, the wire was light blue. When the fish returned three or four years later, the insulation had dissolved, leaving only bare, stainless steel wire. We could easily read the codes."

"Perfect," said Mr. Yagi with a smile.

Following a tour of the factory, Akio left for his hotel. Because of a sixteen-hour time zone difference between Tokyo and Vancouver, he waited until the next morning to call Gwen.

Excited to give Gwen the news, he talked rapidly, "Gwen, you were right. A substance coating the wires was released into the fish during the ocean phase. Murakami labeled it as the vitamin, folic acid. It must have been something else, some other chemical which acted like a key to unlock the engineered gene."

32. The Discovery

ANOTHER PIECE NOW FIT INTO THE PUZZLE. MURAKAMI'S TRACKER wire contained a substance which awakened *Lamda's* engineered gene from its sleeping state. When the wire's insulation dissolved in the ocean, activating-solution entered the salmon's body, unlocking the gene which fixed *Lamda* in its prime of life.

By now Gwen held a full-time research and teaching job at CU. Hoping to prove this theory, she submitted a research plan to CU's Molecular Biology Department for approval. Because of restrictions against altering ova, they rejected her first proposal. By substituting coho fibroblasts for ova, her study gained approval. She used fibroblasts because they're abundant cells in mammals and salmon. They grow into the connective tissue responsible for building a body's supporting scaffolding.

Despite a year attempting to grow salmon fibroblast cells without success, Gwen persisted in trying to uncover the mystery hidden in *Lamda's* altered gene. One cold winter afternoon, Akio visited her in the lab, hoping to lure her out to a movie or dinner.

"Aki, take a look at the Petri dishes in the incubator."

He saw multiple glass dishes containing nutrients and growing cells. "Some of your cell cultures are thriving. What are you feeding them? The agar doesn't look tasty to me."

Maintaining a serious face, she said, "Those are the coho fibroblasts I told you about. They're growing in three different sets of Petri dishes. In each, I count the number of times the cells divide until they stop."

"You're comparing them with the Hayflick limit?" Akio asked.

171

Although Akio had chosen the mushroom business and teaching Japanese over scientific research, the Hayflick limit remained fresh in his mind. He remembered Dr. Hayflick had discovered that human fibroblasts growing in tissue culture would divide about fifty times before stopping. His observation showed healthy cells have a finite lifespan.

"I compared the three sets of growing fibroblasts. The first group contains growing fibroblast cells from a normal male coho. They divided about fifty times before stopping," said Gwen.

"Interesting, the same as the Hayflick limit in human fibroblasts," commented Akio.

"Yes, I engineered the second group's fibroblasts by replacing their normal ATPase promoter gene with a copy of *Lamda's* altered one. They also divided about fifty times before stopping."

"As expected, they acted as normal cells because their modified gene was locked and silent," said Akio.

"Correct. Now, look at group three. These Petri dishes contain the same genetically altered cells as in group two, but received the activator solution after thirty normal divisions."

"Activator solution, such as the one on the CWT wire? Where did you find that?" questioned a surprised Akio.

"I made it."

He raised his eyebrows in disbelief, "You made it?"

"Yes, I made it. Knowing the normal coho genome, and having cells from *Lamda*, I copied *Lamda's* engineered promoter gene. Reconstructing the activator protein was as routine for me as it would be for a locksmith to make a new key from a lock's template. I constructed the solution from the altered gene's template."

Akio paused to think about the process she was describing. "Nice work! You added activator at thirty divisions to simulate

Lamda's prime of life age in the ocean. How many times did those cells divide?"

In a slow, subdued tone, Gwen answered, "They're still dividing, now over two hundred times." With a pained expression, she waited for Akio's reaction.

The enormity of Gwen's discovery hasn't yet hit Akio. He thought out loud, "Your activator solution unlocked the silent gene in *Lamda's* fibroblasts, releasing the man-made promoter gene's ability to defy aging. Since ATP declines with aging, keeping ATP at its prime of life level kept *Lamda* forever young."

Akio now understood. They looked at each other in silence. What had been only a theory about a fish that defied aging had become a reality. A sickening feeling replaced the joy expected from both young scientists who had just made a significant discovery.

"What have I done, Aki?" She looked down at the floor, shaking her head in disbelief. "Aging and death are essential for the survival of a species. They're necessary ingredients in Darwin's recipe for all life. Have I just entered an area of science where no human should go?"

Bundled in their coats, they left the lab and started walking. They crossed the campus in silence, walked along trails through Spanish Banks, gazed at the water of English Bay, and followed the shore through Jericho Park. Deep in thought, Gwen walked past her boat club without giving it a glance.

Not until they turned toward home did she break the silence, "Now we know who, what, and how, but we don't know why."

"Yes, looks like Okawa and Murakami created *Lamda*," said Akio. "Okawa worked alone in his private lab engineering eggs supplied to him from Fukahori's hatchery. After several experimental batches failed, he created the what, a modified gene capable of stopping aging at the prime of life. You recreated the how by duplicating Okawa's method in the lab." Aki's emphasis on the word you caused a blast of breath to condense against the cold air.

"And Murakami, how do you think he fit in?" Gwen asked.

"When Japan's application to participate in the Joint Canadian Project landed on his desk, he must have felt he had received a divine gift. His aging experiments had suffered from a dwindling number of cohos returning to Japan. Their abundance in Canada solved his problem."

"Why do you think he devised a study about homing instincts and not aging?" Gwen asked.

"He needed an irresistible sales pitch to gain entrance into the study. It masked his real intention to field-test his anti-aging research."

"And all the secrecy?"

"Murakami and Okawa knew Japan and Canada frowned upon gene-editing experiments on reproductive cells," said Akio, "They had to work in secret."

"What could be more unethical than using a joint international research project for personal gain?" questioned Gwen.

"Maybe labeling his gene activator as a vitamin."

"They had lots to keep secret. They both turned out to be slimy and ingenious. How did you fit into their plan?" asked Gwen.

"Murakami stumbled upon me. Okawa must have sent him our dissertation on ATP. Being knowledgeable about ATP, fluent in Japanese and English, and educated in Canada, I fit into his scheme. The salary fit into mine."

"They used you to legitimize their study. Our dissertation concepts about ATP helped them devise their method. How do you feel about that?"

"Used," he sighed. "I was unaware of this information while I directed the project in Canada."

"Why do you think they wanted to create *Lamda*?" asked Gwen.

The question went unanswered. Two young scientists found themselves sitting on the cusp between science fiction and reality. In college, both had read Jules Verne's 1885 novel about men traveling to the moon. H.G. Wells followed in 1900, writing about the same dream which at the time was thought to be impossible. Talking watches, airplanes, rocket ships, robots, laser beams, and driverless cars existed only in the fantasies of dreamers and in the pens of writers. Fish that don't age?

Immortality?

Fiction?

Maybe not. . . .

33. Why

GWEN AND AKIO'S CONVERSATION CONTINUED IN THEIR apartment. A bottle of wine stood within reach of their sofa in readiness for whatever their discussion might uncover.

Since the Japanese vote reaffirming a male-only right to the Throne passed, Akio had been doing his research. Having kept a close watch on public records from Japan, he was able to construct a timeline.

"Take a look at my timeline," he asked Gwen as he pointed to a list of dates and events he had constructed on his laptop. "It starts here in 1985 when Dr. Okawa joined the Imperial Institute of Genetics as Director of In Vitro Science."

Gwen leaned over for a better look. Akio continued, "Let's skip ahead to 2003. The aging Crown Prince and Princess had little time left to bear more children. They had one daughter and no sons. I think the Royal couple approached Okawa about storing their eggs and sperm in the Institute's bank in case they were needed in the future. As director of the in vitro program at the Institute and as a loyal subject of the Crown, Okawa carried out their wishes.

"Moving ahead to 2005, we see Okawa retired from the Institute to start GenLife. Murakami took over his position at the Institute of Genetics. Murakami now had total control over the Royal Family's stored gametes and embryos."

Akio pointed to another entry recorded between the time Gwen caught her *Lamda* and the vote determining ascension to the throne. "I located the minutes the government released from political meetings held during the year before the vote. This one caught my attention."

Akio filled their glasses from their bottle of chardonnay. "The release didn't include minutes, only the name of the group and the attendees."

"What caught your eye?'

"Okawa and Murakami attended the Party of Amaterasu's meeting.

"Meaning?"

"Their party is regarded as ultraconservative, known for interpreting Japanese myth as fact. They believe the Emperor is Divine and should always be male. Their party lobbied the Diet to vote against a woman's right to ascend to the Throne. Other records showed Murakami and Okawa contributed large sums of money to the party."

"This still doesn't answer the question why they created *Lamda*."

"Hold the thought. Look several months after the vote legalizing in vitro and surrogacy. Records from the Imperial House report an in vitro fertilization took place on an unidentified Royal surrogate. Being the Director of In Vitro Sciences for the entire Royal family, Murakami delivered the fertilized eggs to the operating room. Nine months after the procedure, the Royal surrogate gave birth to a healthy son, Prince Hitomu. Since his father, the Crown Prince, had become Emperor two months before, Prince Hitomu is now heir to the Chrysanthemum Throne."

"You're saying because the Crown Princess was unable to bear another child, the Royal couple asked Murakami to use their stored ova and sperm for in vitro fertilization in a surrogate?"

"Yes, perfectly legal except I think Murakami may have genetically engineered her ova before fertilizing them with her husband's sperm. Next, he selected a male embryo with an altered X chromosome to implant into the surrogate."

Shaking her head in disbelief, Gwen gasped, "It can't be!"

"That's my theory," said Akio, in an apologetic tone. "Murakami and Okawa used their *Lamda* technology to modify the Crown Princess's ova. The Canadian Project was their trial run for the procedure. Since the in vitro took place several years after *Lamda*, they had plenty of time to learn how to adapt *Lamda* technology to human ova."

Gwen's shifted restlessly to find a more comfortable position on the couch, as her thoughts reflected her discomfort about where this theory was leading.

Akio continued, "I believe Murakami timed the in vitro procedure on the Royal surrogate to occur after the affirmative vote legalized their use. To prevent a discovery of his genetic manipulation of *Lamda*, he delayed the release of the coho genome until after Prince Hitomu was born."

"You think Murakami, with help from Okawa, took the Crown Princess's stored ova, altered the ATPase promoter gene, and fertilized them with the Crown Prince's stored sperm. Do you think the Crown Prince ordered Murakami do this?" asked Gwen shaking her head in disbelief.

"Not a chance, only Okawa and Murakami had access to the Royal embryos. Not needing or wanting anyone else, they acted alone. The Royals are honorable people. If Murakami had asked for permission to alter the couple's genes, they would have said no, ending the scheme. Okawa and Murakami couldn't take the risk. They felt compelled to seize this opportunity to further their own political and religious aims."

"Which ones?"

"They're fanatics, complete throw-backs to pre-World War II thinking. They consider the myth of the sun goddess to be fact. They distort Shinto to justify their goals. They believe the Emperor is Divine and consider the Japanese a superior race. Out of the batch of altered embryos, they selected a male, ensuring a male would occupy the Throne after the Reigning Emperor dies."

Still shaking her head in disbelief, Gwen said, "What do you think will happen next?"

"Prince Hitomu now carries the silent, modified gene. Similar to *Lamda*, he will develop normally. Sometime between the ages of eighteen and twenty-two, he'll receive an injection of activator."

"And who will give him the shot?"

"I predict it will be Dr. Murakami's son who is Prince Hitomu's pediatrician. Remember, a sworn promise to one's father is sacred in Japan. Without knowing the shot's content or intent, I think Murakami's son made a promise to his father."

After Gwen shook the last few drops of wine from the bottle, and with a tone of resignation, she said, "Their plot ensured a male would always be Emperor. Immortal male coho, immortal fibroblast, immortal male Emperor—a symbol of the rising sun forever."

34. Ethics

GWEN SPENT A FITFUL NIGHT. MANY THOUGHTS ROILED IN HER mind's pot of confusion. A battle waged between the pros and cons of continuing her immortality research. While on a weekend fishing trip with her father, she had stumbled on a fish that didn't age. Compelled by her fear of death, she used modern technology to uncover the science behind *Lamda*. Despite nearing her goal, she felt conflicted over a potential victory against her nemesis, death.

Except for Dr. Trisha Browning, Gwen had only confided her thanatophobia with Akio.

"What's your advice, Aki? Should I continue researching immortality or bury it?

Akio had to think for a moment how he should answer his wife's question. He felt immortality could be as detrimental to life as nuclear weapons. He also respected his wife's battle with her fear of death and thought the answer should be hers.

"Start by asking yourself a basic question: Is gene editing of sperm and ova ethical?"

A simple question left Gwen stumped by its complexity. She thought out loud, "Um, well, in the future, maybe, maybe not. I guess if a person carried an abnormal gene causing a serious disease, substituting it with a normal gene would improve that person's life."

Akio asked, "Since changes made in germ cells are passed down to future generations, when should they not be used?"

Gwen thought and answered, "When inherited changes modify evolution in a negative way."

"Such as?"

Despite feeling a little uneasy not knowing why Akio was asking these questions, she enjoyed being taken back to the questions debated in her scientific ethics course at school.

Gwen answered, "A wealthy parent wants her next son to be the world's fastest runner. She orders a new gene capable of boosting muscle power. It's inserted into her ova. Over generations, the gene will pollute the entire human genome. That genetic alteration would be unethical."

"Knowing the human genetic code took three and one-half billion years to create, is modifying genes to create immortality ethical?"

Gwen stumbled again, "Well, ah, ah, in Okawa's and Murakami's case; it wasn't ethical."

"And in yours?"

She thought back to the immortality exhibit she had seen years ago at the expo. She saw a world filled with stifling monotony, a population of only young and middle-aged people, the absence of the seniors' wisdom and youth's fresh ideas, a world where a lottery would determine which lucky few could have a baby. On a scientific level, she understood genetic alterations designed to eliminate death would present an existential threat to all life as we know it. Spontaneous mutations occurring during the years when people procreate are the driving forces of evolution. Without a viable new gene pool, a species would cease to evolve. Eliminating natural selection from humans would open the door for replacement by a fitter species. Despite knowing death is an indispensable component of evolutionary survival, her fear of death still fought in a tug-of-war against her scientific knowledge.

She circumvented Akio's question about the ethics of her research. "I think I've told you about the expo I visited during my undergraduate years. I remember walking out of the pessimistic immortality exhibit, thinking, I'd still rather live a few thousand years and see for myself. For now, the closer my research brings me to the possibility of achieving human immortality, the worse I feel about it."

"Would knowing it's too late for you to become immortal change your opinion? When your mother's ovum was fertilized, the moment you became an embryo, your death sentence was sealed. To achieve immortality with the *Lamda* method, altering your mother's ovum had to happen before conception. You're too late for immortality. Your decision to continue researching immortality is no longer about you. It's about what's best for life on Earth."

Akio's words stunned her. Had Akio hit upon the root cause of her phobia? She had never thought about her quest for immortality as selfishness.

"Are you saying not accepting death is narcissistic?"

Akio didn't answer the question. It hung in silence until he continued, "Does discovering the answer to immortality contribute to the common good of our species?"

"Are you saying you think continuing my research into immortality would be as unethical as Okawa's and Murakami's?"

Akio said, "I think Okawa and Murakami must have struggled with a similar dilemma. To achieve their goal, they had to breach their scientific ethics. They broke laws concerning germ cell modification. Their obsessive political and religious beliefs compelled them to ensure a male Emperor would be immortal. They betrayed the trust of the Royal Family they served. To give them some credit, they compromised. Instead of selling immortality to the highest bidder or keeping it for their own families, they restricted their discovery to creating one immortal human, Prince Hitomu. After his birth, they buried their research. If their method works, when he receives the promoter solution, only Prince Hitomu will stop aging. Hopefully, the activator vial used on him will be the last. Okama and Murakami will take their secret to their graves."

Gwen saw her situation's similarity with Murakami's, except her motivation wasn't religious or political. Her motivation was her fear of death. As tears formed, she said, "My goal of immortality is selfish. I know we should let the secret die with us, but I'm still torn."

Akio took her hand, "Forever is a long time. We both know immortality is an impossible goal. We can't avoid death. Even if aging stops, mortality doesn't. The immortal *Lamdas* died from natural causes within a few years. Immortal humans eventually would meet the same fate. Why worry about something unavoidable? Worrying about it is self-destructive."

"How do I stop worrying?"

"Accept all living things will eventually die, including you and I and everyone we love. Concern yourself with living, not worrying about dying."

Akio's words gave Gwen a sense of relief she'd thought could only come from discovering the secret to immortality. Continuing to hold her hand, he said, "We can do this together."

Deep in thought, she looked down. In a soft voice, she said, "Two men, acting alone, peacefully developed a powerful weapon capable of destroying human life on earth. If we're correct, they settled for a symbolic gesture. After the last dose of activator is given to Prince Hitomu, their secret method will die— like *Lamda*, Murakami, Okawa, the Emperor's progeny, you, and me."

35. Three Years Later

"Rat-a-tat-tat, rat-a-tat-tat" resounded from the first row of drummers. The parade celebrating the opening of Three Peaks Mushroom, Inc.'s new building started punctually, thirty minutes late. With its siren blaring and lights flashing, a tribal police car led the procession.

Akio and Gwen had flown in from Vancouver on this warm day in early May. They came to join the celebration and to show off their four-month-old daughter, Harriet Frances Naiporo. Three years had passed since they uncovered *Lamda's* secrets. Gwen had buried all footprints left by her research and judging by the silence coming out of Japan, Okawa and Murakami had done the same. One week after Prince Hitomu's birth, Okawa sold GenLife. Six months later, at the age of seventy-six, he became chairman of the Party of Amaterasu. Murakami retained his position as chief of the in vitro division at the Imperial Institute of Genetics. He planned on retiring in two years. His son headed the Royal Household's Pediatrics Department where one of his patients, Crown Prince Hitomu, continued to develop normally.

Back in Three Peaks, wearing blue and gold uniforms, Regional High's marching band followed the tribal police cruiser. Tubas, flutes, trumpets, and trombones synchronized behind the drums. The band's only clarinet player missed the parade because of a work conflict. Next came a pickup truck carrying Fred Stevens. The fifty-year-old Chief of Three Peaks Band Council, wearing a light sport coat and jeans, held onto the cargo bay with one hand while waving with the other. Next came a fire truck. A familiar person gripped the engine's side rail. "Peter," yelled his mother as he passed by their house. Gwen's little brother had grown up and found his dream job. He was now Chief Financial Officer and General Manager of Three Peaks Mushroom. Clutching onto him stood Tommy Teegee, still everyone's favorite. He wore a fire department helmet and sported a badge designating him honorable firefighter of the day.

As the parade passed by houses, interested occupants joined in at the end of the procession. While Mary and Gwen pushed little Harriet in her baby carriage, Akio and Frank blended in with the other walkers in the rear of the procession. Although he founded the business, Frank tried to avoid his deserved but unwanted accolades.

The parade passed by Big Bill Gwiniti's house. This aging pillar of the community sat rocking on his porch, frustrated by his physical inability to join the parade. Still defying all odds by remaining alive, little Bill Gale stood on his porch, giving the thumbs down sign to anyone who would look. He refused to work with the mushroom project because, as he was heard to say more than once, "No damn plot by the Canadian government is gonna control me." He still continued to accept all the benefits given to him by his perceived enemy.

Playing the high school's fight song, the band marched past the elementary school, the traditional feast hall, and a kaleidoscope of simple houses. Joe Blackstone's condemned house awaited demolition. He lived in prison now, where he'll spend at least twenty years more years for the attempted murder of his ex-wife. His daughter, Skyla, bounced between half-way houses and drug rehabilitation centers. When Gwen pushed her baby carriage in front of Karen's house, another of her jump-roping friends, Karen ran across the yard to greet her. A pure-bred, Indigenous woman, Karen married a non-Indigenous man and moved to Toronto to pursue a career in software engineering. She had come

185

to visit her parents for the weekend.

The parade continued to zig-zag through the reserve's maze of dirt roads. It passed the Catholic church, Skeena Elementary, the small library, and the medical clinic, before coming to a halt in front of the new mushroom processing plant's main doors. A long blue ribbon blocked its entrance. Behind the ribbon stood a smiling, Chief Stevens and Peter. Each held a pair of large shears.

The Chief spoke first, "When Frank Sunrise gave us the idea of expanding his small mushroom business model, the Council doubted it would work. We predicted government regulations wouldn't permit it. Frank persisted. He wanted to form a bigger mushroom business owned and staffed by people of our Three Peaks Nation. Two reasons persuaded us to grant him a three year trial period. First, over his six decades of service to our Nation, every time we disagreed with Frank, we were wrong. Second, he didn't ask for money." The Chief laughed along with the audience. "By citing the precedents established in the Delgamuukw Case of 1998, which granted Aboriginal land rights for hunting and fishing on the land we claim, Frank talked the Department of Forestry into granting us permission to proceed. With the enthusiasm of our community, a rundown old barn, three abandoned trucks, and hours of work, our own Frank Sunrise laid the foundation for Three Peaks Mushroom.

"Our reserve has spent much of its daily life in financial struggle. The mushroom business is doing for us what casinos have done for other Nations. Our business is owned and staffed by us. Our community's self-esteem has risen. Half the employable people living on the reserve have found work in some capacity within the company. As a non-profit organization, all profits are reinvested back into the Nation in the form of increased salaries and community development. Other local reserves have joined us."

186

The Chief stopped to acknowledge Frank in the crowd. When the applause subsided, he continued, "Before cutting the ribbon, let's hear from Peter Sunrise, a resident of Three Peaks and the brains behind our finances. He'll update us about the business's long-range plans."

As if giving a political speech, Peter bellowed, "This new building will double our output and create more jobs. Now we can expand to markets overseas. Thanks to Akio Naiporo's part ownership in Hokkaido Mushroom, we'll be their only foreign supplier of matsutakes. Akio is now in the process of converting their plant in Japan into an Ainu business patterned after ours. The Ainu people in Japan are also an Indigenous People with a long history of forced assimilation and discrimination, not all that different then our own. I predict our Native-to-Native business will continue to expand, and maybe, just maybe, we'll add smoked salmon to the product list."

With Native and Canadian press photographers snapping pictures, Frank joined Chief Stevens and Peter in cutting the ribbon. The Chief raised his hands over his head and yelled, "Let's get to work."

The Sunrise family walked home to prepare a picnic. While Harriet napped in her crib, Mary and Gwen sat down in the shade. "With all the excitement about mushrooms, I sometimes want to relax and think about the big picture," said Mary, gazing up into the sky."

"What picture, Mother?" Gwen asked.

"Our lives. What are they all about?"

"Yours is easy. You've raised two children and spent decades helping students follow their dreams. Isn't that what life is about for you?"

"Yes, I guess it is." Mary smiled.

As the conversation continued, it became apparent Mary

187

wasn't talking about her own life. She wanted Gwen to talk about hers. For a long time, she sensed her daughter struggled with something that had been left unspoken. Not wanting to violate the stoic, Three Peaks reluctance to discuss emotions, she never before broached the subject with Gwen. "Do you think about your own life, what it's all about for you?"

"I do, Mother. My life is about respecting nature and bettering the lives of others, about my husband, family, friends, and now my daughter."

"We're proud of you. What projects are you researching now?"

"I'm testing a chemical called ATPase to see if its energy-enhancing properties could decrease some of the pain associated with aging. Imagine a medicine you could rub on your joints to ease the burden of arthritis?"

Mother acknowledged Gwen by asking, "Since people are living longer, you're trying to help aging become a happier and healthier period of life?"

"After you retire, when your kids are grown, and you're an old woman looking back at your life, what do you think you would have wanted to have changed?" Mother asked.

Gwen never talked to her family about her fear of death. "I would have wanted to believe in a supernatural power who grants good people an eternal life together. You have Catholicism and Father has Indigenous spirituality. I'll regret not having those answers. I can only grasp onto the hope your beliefs will come true."

"Hope for what?"

"Hope we will be together forever."

Mary understood. She stood up from her chair, stroked her daughter's hair, and said, "Death is inevitable. If you allow fear of the unknown to ruin your life, it will. Find your meaning in life. Fill it with improving the world your children will inherit. The rest will take care of itself."

Mother had set up Harriet's crib in Gwen's old room. Gwen slept in the bed beside Harriet, hoping to shield her parents from reliving the sleepless nights they spent during her infancy. Akio slept in Peter's old bedroom across the hall.

The same night, between breast-feedings, Gwen had a vivid dream. Although she had learned dreams consist of repeating short segments, that theory didn't hold up for this one. In the dream she saw a much older version of herself sitting on the porch steps of her parents' house. She was waiting for her twenty-year-old son, Robbie, to pick her up. On her sixty-second birthday, she had broken her leg in a bicycle accident. Although on the mend, she still needed a cane for balance. Robbie volunteered to drive her to the tribal burial grounds for a visit.

Displaying a 2044 registration sticker on his license plate, his dented red pickup truck backed down the muddy driveway towards the porch stairs where his mother was waiting. He jumped out, waving a Japanese newspaper.

"Look, Mother, interesting news from Japan."

Robbie studied Japanese in college and had become fluent by talking with his father. He pointed to a picture of Prince Hitomu on the front page.

"What does it say?" asked Gwen.

"The Emperor is dead. Crown Prince Hitomu now sits on the Chrysanthemum Throne."

"Sad news. The Emperor suffered so long," Gwen sighed. "But look at Prince Hitomu. He looks like he's twenty." Gwen smiled when she calculated the new Emperor's age to be thirty-five.

"What are you smiling about, Mother?"

"Oh, nothing, I thought about something that would have

made your father laugh."

Robbie continued reading, "The seemingly ageless new Emperor pledges his love for Japan and its people. He hopes to continue his father's work, promoting peace and prosperity."

Gwen wished Akio was there with her now. She could imagine him looking her in the eye and nodding his head up and down as if to say, "We knew it. We were right. Prince Hitomu carried the altered gene and received the promoter activator in his early twenties."

Robbie helped her into his truck. The old walking trail leading from the trailhead was now a single-lane dirt road pockmarked with mounds of grass. Gwen flashed back to her childhood days when she rode with her father on Gypsy along the same route. The drive to the cemetery took only a few minutes now.

Assisted by Robbie, she walked in silence from the truck to the family plot. They stopped at the simple gravestones of her grandparents, father, mother, and Akio. Her mother died two years ago at age eighty, her father three years before at age eighty-five. Today marked the first anniversary of Akio's death.

Robbie had learned about Three Peaks culture from his grandfather. He lifted his arms towards the sky, looked up, and chanted, "May the spirits of my great grandparents, my grandparents, and my father, live among us, protect us, and guide us through the Circle of Life." Gwen and Robbie embraced and wept.

Her dream flashed back to her life with Akio. She saw herself squeezing his gold wedding band in the palm of her hand. As his fingers and legs swelled from cancer's devastating effects, he removed it for fear of constricting his finger. He died three days later. The wedding band and her memories were all that remained. She remembered placing it on his finger during their wedding ceremony at Three Peaks. It signified an everlasting love, a bond between them that would last forever. She remembered what love was when they were young, more about passion and desires. When their lives became consumed by career and family, they were more partners than lovers. After the children left, their bond became a deep true love. They were glued together, like two attracting magnets. I no longer existed, only we.

Gwen's weeping became louder before changing from her cry to the cry of a baby. She jolted awake to find herself back in her childhood bedroom next to her hungry infant. Across the hallway slept her parents and Akio.

After nursing, Gwen placed Harriet back into the crib. She lulled her baby to sleep by singing a song from her childhood,

> *Row, row, row your boat,*
> *Gently down the stream.*
> *Merrily, merrily, merrily, merrily,*
> *Life is but a dream.*

Made in the USA
Columbia, SC
08 March 2021